Santiago had never wanted a woman this much in his life, and _damn her_ she knew it. He wanted her so badly that he could taste it. He wanted to taste her so badly that... He embraced his anger just to stay in control.

Lucy sucked in a deep, wrathful breath and blurted, 'You manipulative—'

He moved so fast it seemed that one moment he was standing several feet away and the next he was beside her, with his finger poised a whisper away from her parted lips. She felt the pressure building inside and was totally helpless to do anything about it.

'Think very carefully before you continue, Lucy. I am not my brother and I am not in the habit of turning the other cheek.'

'You're—' He lunged without warning and grabbed her by the waist. The other hand went to the nape of her neck, his fingers pushing into her hair as he pulled her into him.

Kim Lawrence lives on a farm in rural Anglesey. She runs two miles daily, and finds this an excellent opportunity to unwind and seek inspiration for her writing! It also helps her keep up with her husband, two active sons, and the various stray animals which have adopted them. Always a fanatical consumer of fiction, she is now equally enthusiastic about writing. She loves a happy ending!

Recent titles by the same author:

GIANNI'S PRIDE*
IN A STORM OF SCANDAL
THE THORN IN HIS SIDE
  (21st Century Bosses)
A SPANISH AWAKENING *(One Night In...)*

*linked to SANTIAGO'S COMMAND

**Did you know these are also available as eBooks?
Visit www.millsandboon.co.uk**

SANTIAGO'S COMMAND

BY
KIM LAWRENCE

First published in Great Britain 2012
by Mills & Boon, an imprint of Harlequin (UK) Limited.
Harlequin (UK) Limited, Eton House, 18-24 Paradise Road,
Richmond, Surrey TW9 1SR

© Kim Lawrence 2012

ISBN: 978 0 263 22784 0

Harlequin (UK) policy is to use papers that are natural, renewable
and recyclable products and made from wood grown in sustainable
forests. The logging and manufacturing process conform to the
legal environmental regulations of the country of origin.

Printed and bound in Great Britain
by CPI Antony Rowe, Chippenham, Wiltshire

SANTIAGO'S
COMMAND

CHAPTER ONE

'Lucy Fitzgerald...?'

Santiago, who had been half listening to his brother's enthusiastic description of the latest woman who was 'the one', lifted his head, the indent above his narrowed eyes deepening as he tried to place the name that seemed for some reason strangely familiar.

'Do I know her?'

At the question his half-brother, who had gone to stand in front of the large gilded mirror above the room's impressive fireplace, laughed. He took one last complacent look at his reflection, ran a hand over the dark hair he wore collar length and turned back to his brother with a white grin. 'Oh, if you'd met Lucy you wouldn't have forgotten,' he promised confidently. 'You'll love her, Santiago.'

'Not as much as you love *you*, little brother.'

Ramon, who, unable to resist the lure of his reflection, had swivelled his gaze to cast a critical look at his profile, dragged a hand over his carefully groomed stubble before responding to the jibe with a joking retort: 'You can always improve upon perfection.'

In reality, Ramon was philosophical that, effort or not, perfect profile or not, he was never going to have what his charismatic brother had and wasted. If not criminal, it was at the very least bad manners to Ramon's way of thinking to not even appear to notice the women who seemed more than willing to overlook his brother's imperfect profile—the slight bump in his nose was a permanent reminder of Santiago's rugby-playing days—as they sought to attract his attention by any, some not exactly subtle, means.

He angled his speculative gaze at the older man seated behind the massive mahogany desk. Despite the fact he wasted opportunities, his brother was no monk, but he was equally by no stretch of the imagination a player.

'Will you ever marry again, do you think?' Ramon regretted the unconsidered words the moment they left his lips. 'Sorry, I didn't mean to...' He gave an awkward shrug. It had been eight years since Magdalena had died and even though he'd been a kid at the time himself Ramon could still remember how awful the dead look in his brother's eyes had been. Even now a careless mention of Magdalena's name could bring it back. Not that he didn't have a constant reminder: little Gabriella was the spitting image of her mother.

Feeling sympathy for Ramon's obvious discomfort, Santiago pushed away the sense of crushing failure and guilt any thought of his dead wife always evoked and made himself smile.

'So this Lucy is making you think of marriage...?' he asked, changing the subject, fully anticipating his brother's horrified denial. 'She must be special,' he drawled.

'She is...'

Santiago's brows lifted at the vehemence in his brother's response.

'Very special. Marriage...?' A thunderstruck expression crossed Ramon's face before he directed a challenging look at his brother and added, 'Why not?' Ramon said, looking almost as shocked to hear himself say the words as Santiago felt hearing them.

Repressing a groan and taking comfort from the shock, Santiago struggled not to react to the challenge.

'Why not?' he drawled, struggling to keep the bite out of his voice as he added, 'Let me see…you're twenty-three and you've known this girl how long?'

'You were twenty-one when you got married.'

Santiago's dark lashes came down in a concealing mesh as he thought, *And look how well that worked out.*

Aware that too much opposition would just make his brother dig his heels in, Santiago gave an offhand shrug. Ramon's enthusiasms frequently cooled as quickly as they surfaced.

'Maybe I should meet this Lucy…?'

The beginnings of a belligerent gleam faded from his easy-going brother's eyes. 'You'll love her, Santiago, you'll see, you won't be able to help yourself. She's perfect! Totally perfect, a…' He moved his hands in an expressive curving sweep and gave a sigh. 'A goddess.'

Santiago raised an amused brow at the reverent declaration and, grimacing slightly, ran his thumb down the pile of correspondence designated personal that had been awaiting him on his return.

'If you say so.' His thoughts moving on, he picked up the top envelope and got to his feet, stretching the kinks from his spine as he walked around the big mahogany desk.

'You know I've never met anyone like her before.'

'This Lucy sounds…exceptional.' Santiago, who had never encountered a woman who was either perfect or a goddess, humoured Ramon.

'So you've no objection?'

'Bring her to dinner on Friday?'

'Seriously? Here?'

Santiago nodded absently as he scrolled down the page

he held, squinting to read the neat but microscopic tightly packed writing on it. The message it held was familiar: Ramon, his mother said, had messed up and what, she wanted to know, was he going to do about it?

His head lifted. 'You didn't mention you have to retake your second year.' A fact that his stepmother, without actually saying so, managed to expertly imply was actually Santiago's fault.

Maybe, he mused, she had a point?

Had the time come for some tough love? While he wanted his brother to enjoy the freedom he had missed out on after their father's premature death, had he been guilty of overcompensating and being too indulgent and overprotective?

Ramon shrugged. 'To be honest, marine biology isn't really what I was expecting.'

Santiago's jaw tightened as he scanned the younger man's face with narrowed eyes. 'Neither, as I recall, was archaeology or, what was it…ecology…?'

'Environmental science,' his brother supplied. 'Now that, believe me, was—'

'You're so bright, I just don't understand how…' Santiago interrupted, reining in his frustration with difficulty and asking, 'Did you actually go to any lectures, Ramon?'

'A couple…yeah, I know, Santiago, but I'm going to buckle down, really I am. Lucy says—'

'Lucy?' He saw his brother's face and added, 'The goddess. Sorry, I forgot.'

'A good education, Lucy says, is something that no one can take away from you.'

Santiago blinked. This Lucy didn't sound like any of the numerous females his brother had hooked up with to date. 'I'm looking forward to meeting this Lucy.' Maybe a good woman, someone who thought education was a good thing, was what his brother needed?

The jury was still out but he decided to keep an open mind.

When on her very first day at the *finca* Harriet's car had refused to start Lucy had said no problem and walked the mile into town. There had been a problem—not the distance, but the scorching Andalusian midday sun.

A week later Harriet's car was still sitting propped up on bricks in the yard, awaiting the part the mechanic had had to order, and the tip of Lucy's nose was still peeling, though the painful redness had subsided and her complexion had regained its normal pale peaches and cream glow.

Today she had not taken up Harriet's sensible suggestion of a taxi—she loved to walk—but she had chosen a more appropriate time to make the trip and, arriving early, she had managed to buy everything on Harriet's shopping list while it was still cool enough to enjoy the walk back through truly incredible scenery, but she was taking no chances. Lucy had plastered on the factor thirty and borrowed a shapeless straw sun hat from Harriet.

It was still only ten-thirty when she reached the footbridge across the stream that bordered Harriet's property, a single-story terracotta-roofed cottage that had the basics and not much else. It was the four acres of scrubby land that had attracted her friend. On retirement Harriet had decided to live her dream and start, to the amazement of her academic ex-work colleagues, a donkey sanctuary in Spain.

When Lucy had said she thought she was being very brave, her old university tutor had retorted she was simply following the example of her favourite ex-student. Lucy, who was not accustomed to being held up as a role model, had not pointed out that her change of lifestyle had not been one of choice, more of necessity.

On impulse she walked down the grassy bank by the bridge and slipped off her sandals. The first initial touch of the icy water against her hot, dusty skin made her gasp. She laughed with pleasure as she felt her way carefully over the smooth stones, wading out until the water reached her calves.

Pulling off the sun hat, she shook free her ash-blonde hair and, head tipped back to the azure sky, she closed her eyes to shut out the sun and sighed. It was bliss!

With a tightening of his thighs against leather and solid flesh Santiago urged the responsive animal out of the protective shadow of the pine trees where they had paused. His strong-boned features set in an austere, contemplative mask, he patted the animal's neck as it responded to his light touch and walked forward, hooves silent on the boggy patch of ground as they moved towards the fast-flowing stream.

Now he knew why the name had seemed so familiar.

The disguise of sexy angel was good but not that good, not for someone who possessed a once-seen-never-forgotten quality, and Lucy Fitzgerald definitely did!

She was not dressed in the sharp tailored red suit and spiky heels—four years ago that iconic image had been used again and again by the media—but he had no doubt that this was the same woman who had elicited universal condemnation from a morally outraged public.

She hadn't said a word to defend herself, but then that had been the idea; a word that broke the gagging injunction would have landed her in jail, a place that Santiago for one would have paid good money to see her end up!

An image of the tear-stained face of the wronged wife in the story drifted into his head, the brave face the woman put on not hiding the emotional devastation that presented a dramatic contrast to the cold composure that Lucy Fitzgerald had displayed under the camera lens.

It had been the sort of story that under normal circumstances Santiago would not have read beyond the first line—but for the timing. The situation of the advertising executive who had resorted to the courts to protect himself from Lucy Fitzgerald had borne an uncanny resemblance to the one he had at the time found himself in, albeit on a lesser scale.

In his case the woman—he barely remembered her name, let alone her face—who had sought to gain financially had been more opportunistic than ruthless, and of course not being married and caring very little what the world thought of him had made him a less vulnerable target than Lucy Fitzgerald's victim, who, instead of caving in to his mistress's threat of exposure, had instead sought an injunction to stop her speaking out.

Blackmail was the action of a coward and a woman like Lucy Fitzgerald represented everything Santiago despised. This was why, while the face of his own would-be blackmailer, a woman whom he had never even slept with, had vanished, the composed Madonna-like face that had hidden a dark heart of stone had stuck in his mind—his heavy-lidded glance dropped—as had her body.

You and the rest of the male population!

The silent addition caused his firm, mobile lips to twitch into a self-mocking grimace as his dark gaze continued to slide over the lush curves beneath the simple cotton top and skirt she was wearing. The woman might be poison, but she did have a body that invited, actually demanded, sinful speculation.

Of course she was all too…obvious for his taste, but it was easy now to see why his easily influenced brother had been so smitten, a case of lust not love.

Exert a positive influence!

He choked back a bitter laugh. His uncharacteristic and misguided optimism could not have been more poorly timed. Positive? If Lucy Fitzgerald was even a fraction as bad as her reputation, she was toxic!

Santiago felt a passing stab of nostalgia for the empty-headed, pretty but basically harmless party girls his brother had up to this point needed saving from...not that he had saved him. Up to this point Santiago had not ridden to the rescue, deciding that his brother would learn from experience. This, he reflected soberly, was an entirely different situation; he could not allow his brother to become a victim of this woman.

Had she specifically targeted Ramon?

Santiago, who did not believe in coincidence any more than he believed in fate, considered it likely; he could see how his brother would seem an easy prey to someone like her.

Did Ramon know who she was? Did he know about her history or at least her sanitised version of it where she no doubt became the innocent victim? He had no doubt that she could be very convincing and Ramon was obviously completely bewitched, though why bother raking up your sordid past when your victim had still been a teenager when the story had been big news.

A teenager!

Anger flashed in his deep-set eyes, the fine muscle along his angular jaw quivered and clenched beneath the surface of his golden skin. Not only was she a mercenary, corrupt gold-digger, she was a cradle snatcher. She had to be, what...? Doing the maths in his head, he scowled. Thirty, give or take a year or two?

Though admittedly, he conceded, reining in his mount a few feet from the riverbank, she looked younger, and for once in his life his little brother had not exaggerated. Lucy Fitzgerald was a woman that *goddess* could legitimately be used to describe. Poison to the core but breathtakingly beautiful, even barefooted and wearing a simple cotton skirt. On anyone else he would have assumed the transparency that revealed the silhouette of her long shapely thighs under direct sunlight was accidental, with this woman he was willing to bet that even her dreams were contrived.

As she remained oblivious to his presence Santiago took the opportunity to study the genuinely goddess-like attributes beneath the thin fabric.

There was plenty to study. She was tall and statuesque with long legs and a figure of iconic hourglass proportions. The woman oozed sex and Santiago felt a stab of annoyance as, independent of his brain, his body reacted with indiscriminate lust to the image.

As he watched she slid a hand under the neck of her top and wriggled to catch the bra strap that had slipped over her shoulder. The innately sexy action made her suddenly less pin-up and more earthily warm, desirable woman—very desirable.

As the sun caught her waist length hair, turning it to spun silver, Santiago realised that if he wanted to save his brother from this witch's machinations he would have to act swiftly. She was fatally beautiful.

One day Ramon would thank him.

The polished leather of his saddle creaked as he swung his leg over it and leapt lightly to the ground, his booted feet making contact with the stones with a metallic click.

Lucy jumped like a startled deer, instinctive fear showing in her blue eyes as she turned, seeing for a split second the tall, threatening bulk of a male figure outlined against the sun. The correspondingly massive horse beside him was drinking from the stream.

When the man spoke a moment later she had regained control, if not of her banging heart, at least of her expression.

'Sorry, did I startle you?'

Only half to death, Lucy thought, her eyes widening fractionally in reaction to the sound of his voice. The intruder spoke perfect English. He was not English though, she decided, picking up on the faint foreign inflection in his richly textured voice—a voice that was velvet over gravel.

Low in her belly things shifted slightly in response to the tactile quality in that deep voice. Shading her eyes, she gave a faint smile and moved her head in a negative gesture.

'I didn't know anyone... I didn't hear you.' She made a conscious effort to erase the frozen mask that her expression had automatically settled into, the same expression that had earned her the 'ice bitch' tag. It was a struggle; the defensive action was by now deeply ingrained.

There had been a time when she had been in danger of allowing her experiences to make her hard, cynical and— according to her mother—too scared to live. The worried accusation had shaken Lucy and she had been trying very hard of late not to assume the worst in any given situation.

Caution was another matter and in the circumstances seemed only sensible!

Arm crooked to hold back her hair from her face, she waded towards the riverbank, her gaze fixed on her feet to avoid stumbling on the rocky riverbed.

Reaching dry ground, she climbed the slight incline that brought her level with the stranger and close enough, thanks to the prevailing wind, for her nostrils to twitch in response to the scent of leather and horse. She kept her distant smile in place and tilted her head up to look at him.

It was a lot of tilting. He was extremely tall; broad of shoulder, narrow of hip and long of leg. She had an impression of power, raw and elemental. She lifted a hand to shade her eyes and her smile faded as, minus the direct dazzle, the man's face became more than a dark blur.

There was definitely nothing blurred about features that looked as though they had been freshly carved in bronze by the hand of an artist more interested in conveying a masculine ideal than reality. The rider's face, bisected by an aquiline, masterful nose, was long with a broad, intelligent forehead, strong square jaw and high, dramatically chiselled cheekbones. Her gaze drifted to his mouth and paused. It was wide and sculpted, the upper lip firm, the lower sensually full.

It was all jaw-dropping and deep-intake-of-breath stuff. Aware she had been staring and without the faintest clue of how long she had been standing there with her mouth unattractively open, she closed it with a snap and felt an embarrassed flush wash over her skin, struggling to maintain eye contact with the deep-set, heavy-lidded eyes that returned her gaze.

She was an expert at hiding her feelings, but this man took impenetrable to another level entirely. His obsidian stare was totally unreadable. His eyes were incredible; framed by thick ebony lashes that were long and spiky, they were densely dark and flecked with silver. They made her think of a starlit night sky.

Starlit skies…? She resisted the temptation to roll her eyes and thought, *Lucy, girl you need a sugar hit.* Sugar was not what her best friend, Sally—never afraid to call a spade a spade—had said she needed when she had told her she was off to Spain.

'The fact is, Lucy, principles are great and true love is nice and all—but in fairy tales! How about a compromise while you're waiting for your prince to climb your ivory tower? Enjoy a bit of head-banging sex with a sexy Spaniard. Let's face it, you won't be short of offers… God, if I looked like you…'

Lucy, who knew nothing about head-banging sex except

that it wasn't for her, pushed away the memory of the conversation, but not before her glance slid to the sensual contours of the stranger's mouth. She found herself almost envying her friend's pragmatic approach to sex as heat flashed through her in a warm squirmy mess. She cleared her throat but it didn't stop her voice sounding husky and breathless as she said the first thing that came into her head.

'How did you know I was English?'

The last time she'd experienced this knee-sagging, heart-thudding sensation the cause had been an earthquake that had made the hotel rock and brought a nearby chandelier crashing to the floor! Was this what people called animal magnetism? Well, whatever it was he had it! And the earthy aura of maleness was not something she would choose to be this close to.

The stranger soothed his horse with a casual pat of his hand on the glossy flank and raised a satiric brow as he allowed his gaze to sweep down her tumbling waist-length hair in an unrealistic but eye-catching pale silvery blonde.

In all the pictures Santiago had seen she had worn her hair in a puritanical elegant chignon that had exposed the swan-like curve of her pale throat and the determined angle of her delicate jaw. Her hairstyle changed, he presumed, depending on what part she was playing, and he could see the tumbling pre-Raphaelite curls appealing to his brother...actually appealing to any man.

'Your colouring is not exactly local...'

His glance moved over the delicate contours of her face. Up close her pale creamy skin had an almost opalescent sheen, the glow of roses on her smooth cheeks not the result of make-up; astonishingly she wore none. Despite her fair colouring her long curling lashes and arched feathery brows were dark. A purist might say her lush, sensuous lips were too full for her delicate features, but even the harshest critic could have found no room for criticism with her eyes. Wide spaced and slightly slanted, they were an astonishing shade of dramatic blue, the electric colour emphasised by the black rim surrounding the iris.

'Oh...' Lucy lifted a hand to her head, tucking a strand of hair behind her ear as she gave a rueful smile, receiving in response a midnight stare. His expression was still shuttered but she was conscious of inexplicable hostility in his body language.

Was it personal or was he like this with everyone? Feeling increasingly antagonistic—the man's people skills could definitely do with some work—Lucy forced a smile as she admitted lightly, 'I suppose I do stick out a little.'

His dark eyes slid the length of her body.

The studied insolence in his stare brought an angry sparkle to her eyes. She fought the impulse to cover herself with her hands. Forget poor people skills—the man's horse had better manners than him.

'And you try so hard to fade into the background.'

A choking sound left her throat. 'Just what is your problem? I'm not trespassing, you know...but you probably are.' He had the look of someone who did not recognise boundaries.

'I am trespassing?' He looked amused by the suggestion. 'I am Santiago Silva.'

'Should I curtsy or bow?' So this was the man who was literally lord of all he surveyed, including the property that Harriet rented. From what her friend had told her, he was 'a great guy'. Odd—Harriet was normally a pretty good judge of character.

Placing a hand on a hip, oblivious to the sexually provocative style of her pose, she watched as his firm sensual mouth lifted at the corners in a smile that did not touch his hard eyes—they held the warmth of a diamond chip as he returned her stare.

'I had no idea we had such a famous—or should that be infamous?—visitor to the area, Miss Fitzgerald.' He saw her flinch and felt a stab of savage satisfaction as he thought, *Gotcha!*

CHAPTER TWO

A FAMILIAR cold, clammy fist tightened in the pit of Lucy's stomach as she felt her expression freeze over. She cursed herself for being surprised that anyone would recognise her here in Spain; like they said, it was a small world and, with the advent of social networking, even smaller.

It didn't matter how many times she told herself that what total strangers chose to think about her was their problem, not hers, it still hurt, and it made her angry that the stares and contemptuous comments had the power to make her want to crawl away into a corner and hide, which according to some was exactly what she had been doing for four years.

Pride enabled her to lift her chin and train her level stare at his face. She was not going to hide any more; she had done nothing wrong. The gagging injunction was long gone; there was no longer anything stopping her telling her side. Nothing but the stubborn conviction that as the innocent victim she shouldn't have to explain to anyone; after all, the people that mattered had never believed any of the lies that had been printed about her.

'If I'd known how warm, charming and welcoming the natives were I would have made it here sooner,' she said, flashing him a smile of saccharine-sweet insincerity and having the satisfaction of seeing his jaw tighten in annoyance.

'And how long are you thinking of staying?'

'Why? Are you planning on running me out of town, sheriff?' she mocked, adopting a mock-Western drawl.

He responded to her levity with another stony stare. On the receiving end, Lucy found the level of his relentless hostility frankly bewildering.

God, does this man need to get a life!

Her story was old news and even if he believed she was as bad as they had painted her, which in truth was pretty bad, it hardly explained an antipathy that seemed...personal?

'I shouldn't joke—you probably can.'

She had the impression that all this man had to do was snap his fingers and the locals would be lining up to be part of a run-her-out-of-town posse, less a form of mob mentality and more mass hypnotism.

She wasn't seeing much evidence of it but it was clear the man exerted some sort of weird charismatic control locally... either that or there was something in the water. In the time she had been here Lucy had heard the name Santiago Silva with monotonous regularity in the area. You couldn't buy a loaf of bread without hearing someone sing the praises of this paragon, which, considering he was a banker—a fairly universally despised animal these days—seemed pretty amazing to Lucy.

Their comments had built an image of someone very different from the man standing there looking down his autocratic nose at her. He did not look remotely like the warm, caring person she'd heard described, but he did look every inch the autocratic feudal throwback who expected people to bow and scrape.

'You have met my brother.' He arched an ebony brow.

A mystified Lucy began to shake her head, then the penny dropped.

Her eyes widened. 'Ramon.' Who had rung the *finca* just before she left that morning inviting her to dinner at the *cas-*

tillo. Wow, was she glad she'd said no to this opportunity to meet his brother…the sort of social event nightmares were made of if this taster was any indicator! Stiff and starchy now, imagine how he'd look in a tie—besides beautiful. Lucy gave her head a little shake to dispel this image.

It was not so surprising she hadn't seen the connection straight off; Ramon had none of the autocratic arrogance of his unpleasant brother. He was actually a really sweet boy who had gone out of his way to help when they had been stranded in the clinic car park the day after she arrived. He'd been a hero, administering first aid to Harriet's ancient car.

Since then he had called twice at the *finca,* the last time, she recalled with a smile, he had helped her catch one of the donkeys before the vet arrived, falling flat on his face in the dust and dirt at one point and ruining his lovely suit. It was hard to believe he was related to this man.

'You will not meet him again.' The comment was delivered in a soft, almost conversational tone that was in stark variance to the menace it conveyed.

Lucy shook her head, genuinely bewildered by the turn this conversation was taking. Was this about her refusing the invitation to dinner at the big house? Had she committed some sort of social faux pas?

The possibility bothered her for Harriet's sake. Her friend had made a lot of effort to fit in so she felt her way cautiously. 'I won't?'

'No, Miss Fitzgerald, you will not.'

'Is Ramon going away?'

'No, you are going away.'

Lucy's patience snapped. 'Will you stop being so damned enigmatic and spit it out? Just what are you trying to say?'

He cut across her in a voice that felt like an icy shower. 'For someone who is clearly a clever woman you have not done your research. Until he is twenty-five, my brother has no access to his trust fund unless I approve it, and I will not. The lifestyle my brother enjoys now is totally at my discretion.'

'Poor Ramon,' she said, feeling sorry for Ramon but not totally sure why his brother should think the information was of interest to her.

'So you will be wasting your time.'

'My time to waste,' she responded, still without the faintest idea what this discussion was about.

The flippancy brought his teeth together in a snarling white smile. 'I suggest you cut your losses and move on to a more profitable…subject.'

Totally at sea now, Lucy shook her head. 'I haven't the faintest idea what you're talking about,' she was forced to admit.

Irritated by this display of innocence, Santiago twisted his expressive mouth in a grimace of fastidious distaste. Sensing his master's mood, the animal at his side pawed the ground and snorted.

Without thinking Lucy responded, moving forward, her hand outstretched to soothe the animal, only to be blocked by the horse's tall rider.

'He does not like strangers.' His concern was for his mount, not the stupid woman who clearly knew nothing about horses.

'Just now I'm identifying with him.'

Santiago was tempted to respond to the challenge gleaming in her blue eyes—the colour was so extraordinary it amounted to an assault on the senses. Instead, he made a decision. 'I want a quick resolution of this situation.'

The solution was not desirable—every cell in his body craved revenge and he was going to reward her but… He breathed a deep sigh, accepting that there were occasions when a man had to do what was necessary as opposed to what was right. He didn't have to like it though.

'If you leave immediately I will cover your expenses.' The resort hotel in the locality was aimed at the high end of the market as it was the only accommodation in the area, barring a couple of rural bed-and-breakfast establishments. He could not imagine the likes of Lucy Fitzgerald roughing it in some rustic retreat—it seemed safe to assume she was a guest at the hotel.

Lucy nodded solemnly and drawled, 'Generous...' Then gave a little laugh and angled a quizzical look at his face. 'But do you think you could give me a clue? I haven't the faintest idea what you're talking about.'

He clicked his tongue irritably. 'Move on, Lucy, you've done innocent and you give a first-class performance, but it tends to pall.'

She pulled herself up to her full height. In most company, even without shoes, that gave her an advantage, but not over this man. Ramon's brother was... Her narrowed glance moved up from his feet—the man was six four easy, possibly more and not an ounce of surplus fat on any of it. He was all hard bone and muscle and enough testosterone to light up the planet.

'My friends call me Lucy.'

'Of which you have many, I am sure,' he cut back smoothly.

Lucy grated her teeth. She had never considered herself a violent person but this man was making her discover new things about herself.

'Expenses and a one-off payment.' His lips curled. What was the going rate for a woman like her these days? 'But only,' he warned, 'if you leave immediately.'

'You want to pay me to leave where exactly?'

'The country and my brother.'

Lucy breathed in and played back the conversation in her head. She could almost hear the sound of the penny dropping. On the outward breath an explosive of anger dumped bucketloads of neat adrenaline into her bloodstream. Lucy saw red, quite literally, she blinked and, still seeing everything through a shimmering red heat haze, linked her badly shaking hands together.

'Let me get this straight. You are offering to pay me to stay away from your brother? I'm curious just how much—no, don't tell me, I might be tempted.'

He did and her eyes widened. 'Wow, you must really think I'm dangerous!'

A nerve pumped beneath the golden-toned skin of his lean cheek but he didn't react to her comment. 'This sum is not negotiable,' he emphasised. 'You must walk away—' He stopped, brows knitting into frustrated lines above his dark eyes. 'What are you doing?'

She paused and threw a look over her shoulder, sticking out one hip to balance the bag she had slung over the other shoulder. 'What am I doing?' She gave a laugh and fixed him with a glittering smile. 'I would have thought that was obvious, Mr Silva—this is me walking. I like walking but nobody has ever offered to pay me for it except for charity. Give me your number and I'll give you a bell the next time I do the marathon.'

He looked so astonished that this time her laugh was genuine.

Santiago watched her make her way up the dusty track, an expression of baffled frustration etched on his handsome face. He had pitched his offer high deliberately; he had allowed for the possibility she might try and negotiate the figure up, but her outright refusal had been an option he had not even considered.

With a gritted oath he vaulted into the saddle and turned his horse in the opposite direction to that she had taken.

It was not until his temper had cooled and he had slowed to a canter that it occurred to him that he had no idea what she had been doing there in the middle of nowhere. The only inhabited building within a two-mile radius was the place he had leased to the English academic who had started up, of all things, a donkey sanctuary.

It would be difficult to imagine two women with less in common, so ruling out that left—what…? Could she have been waiting for someone? In that lonely spot…no…unless… she had been meeting someone and they had required privacy?

By the time the horse had reached the *castillo* gates the conviction that he had stumbled onto a lovers' tryst, that she had been waiting for his half-brother, had become a firm conviction.

His brother was not behaving rationally. Santiago saw those electric-blue eyes in his head and he felt his anger towards his sibling subside. He doubted Ramon was the only man unable to act rationally around Lucy Fitzgerald, who was unable to see past her smouldering sexuality, the only man willing to ignore the truth in order to possess that body, but fortunately for Ramon he was not one of them.

Did she think she had won?

Beneath him Santana responded to the light kick of encouragement and broke into a gallop; to catch a thief one had to adopt the same ruthless methods they did.

Literally shaking with fury, Lucy made the last stage of her journey in record time. She paused at the *finca* door to compose herself. As satisfying as it would have been to vent her feelings on the subject of Santiago Silva, the last thing her friend needed right now was the news that her house guest had had a run in with him.

Harriet would feel obligated to defend her and she could not see that going down well with her feudal despot of a landlord, who would, she thought scornfully, quite likely feel perfectly justified evicting anyone who disagreed with him. He was just the type of small-minded bully who enjoyed wielding the power he had inherited!

No, the best thing all around, she realised, was not to mention the incident at all—and why should she? He had no idea that she was staying with Harriet and so long as she stayed out of his way and she didn't darken his doorstep with her presence—a treat she felt happy to miss out on—unless fate was very unkind she would never have to set eyes on the wretched man again.

Taking comfort from the knowledge, she took a deep breath, pasted on a smile and patted her cheeks. Her eyes widened as she felt the dampness there. God, Santiago Silva had achieved what a media army had failed to do—he had made her cry.

Harriet, normally uncomfortably observant, had not noticed the tear stains, which suggested that her white-faced friend was suffering a lot more than the mild discomfort she claimed after literally hopping out to the stables during Lucy's absence to check on an elderly donkey.

Lucy banned Harriet from attempting any more stunts and hustled her back to bed for a nap. The other woman looked so much better when she rose later that midway through the next morning Lucy suggested another nap and the older woman did not resist the idea.

Lucy decided to use the time to take hay to animals in the scrubby lower pasture. As she walked through the field buzzing with bees and chirruping crickets she became aware of a distant noise disturbing the quiet. As she distributed the feed to the animals who clustered around her the noise got perceptibly closer until… Lucy started and the animals ran at the sound of a loud crash followed by a silence that seemed horribly ominous.

Recovering her wits, Lucy dropped the hay she was holding and ran in the opposite direction to the agitated braying herd. Seconds later, panting, she reached the rise of the slight incline that hid the dirt track below from view and saw the cause of the explosive sound.

Her hand went to her mouth. 'Oh, God!'

One of the modern four-wheel quad bikes was lying at an angle, the front end in a ditch and the back wheels hidden beneath a tangle of scrub that the vehicle had dragged up as it slid off the stony path.

A quick scan revealed no immediate sign of the driver. Had he been thrown clear?

There was no time to speculate. Lucy hit the ground running, scrambling down the rocky incline and raising a cloud of dust from the dry ground. She reached the accident in a matter of seconds, though it felt like a lifetime. There was still no sign of the driver and she couldn't hear anything, but then it was difficult to hear anything above the thundering of her heart in her ears, even her own fearful cry of—

'Is there anyone…? Are you all right?'

'No, I'm not all right. I'm…' A flood of tearful-sounding Spanish preceded a small grunt that was followed by a deep sigh before the young voice added in flawless, barely accented English, 'I'm stuck. Give me a pull, will you?'

Lucy saw the small hand—a child's—appear from beneath the upturned quad bike. She dropped to her knees, her hair brushing the ground as she bent her head to peer underneath. The driver appeared to be a dark-haired young girl.

'It's probably not a good idea to move until—'

'I've already moved. I'm not hurt. It's just my jacket is caught—' The girl gave a small yelp followed by a heartfelt 'Finally!' as she dragged herself out from under the quad bike, emerging beside Lucy looking dusty, in one piece and with nothing but a bloody scrape on the cheek of her heart-shaped face to show for her experience—at least nothing else visible. Lucy remained cautious as the girl, who looked to be around ten or eleven, pulled herself into a sitting position and began to laugh.

'Wow!' Her eyes shone with exhilaration, a reaction that made Lucy think, *God, I'm getting old.* But then, though she'd had her share of her own youthful misadventures, they had had less to do with her being an adrenaline junkie and more to do with her need to please her father and compete with the legendary exploits of her elder siblings.

'That was quite something.'

'I'd call it a lucky escape.' Lucy got to her feet and held out her hand. 'Look, there's no reception here but I really think you should see a doctor to get checked out.'

The girl sprang to her feet energetically, ignoring the extended hand. 'No, I'm fine, I'm…' She stopped, the animation draining from her face as the condition of the overturned vehicle seemed to hit her for the first time. 'Is there any way we could get this back on the road, do you think?'

Lucy shook her head in response to the wistful question. 'I doubt it. I think you should sit down…?' *Before you fall down*, she thought, studying the young girl's pale face.

'Oh, I am in so much trouble. When my dad sees this he'll hit the ceiling. I'm not really meant to ride on this thing…but then I'm not really meant to do anything that is any fun. Do you know what it feels like to have someone act as though you can't even fasten your own shoelace?'

Lucy's lips twitched. 'No, I don't.' If she'd had a penny for every time her dad had said, 'Don't whinge, Lucy, just get on with it,' she would have been able to retire before she hit ten.

'That's why I'm home now, because my dad dragged me away from school. Not that I care. I hate school—he's the one who's always saying how important education is.'

Lucy, who thought so, too, adopted a sympathetic expression as the girl paused for breath, but didn't interrupt as the youthful driver continued in the same if-I-don't-get-it-off-my-chest-now-I'll-explode style.

'And Amelie didn't even have it!'

'Have what?' Lucy, struggling to keep up, asked.

'Meningitis.'

Lucy's brows went up. 'Your school friend has meningitis?'

'No, she doesn't have it, I just said so, and she's not my friend. I have no friends.'

'I'm sure that's not true.'

'It's true, and with a father like mine is it any wonder? He wouldn't let me go on the skiing trip and everyone was going and now, after the head told all the parents that there is no cause for concern, that Amelie didn't have meningitis at all, it was just a virus, what does he do?'

Lucy shook her head, finding she was genuinely curious to know what this much-maligned but clearly caring parent had done.

'Does he listen? No...' she said, pausing in the flow of confidences to turn her bitter gaze on Lucy. 'He lands his helicopter right there in the middle of the lunch break with everyone watching and whisks me off after giving the head an earful. Can you imagine?'

Lucy, who could, bit her quivering lip. 'That must have been dramatic.'

'It was mortifying and now he says I have to go back and there's only two weeks to the end of term.'

'What does your mother say?'

'She's dead.' She stopped, her eyes going round as she turned to face the vehicle hurtling at speed down the hill towards them. It came to a halt with a squeal of brakes feet away from them.

I should have known, Lucy thought as the tall, unmistakeable figure of Santiago Silva exploded from the driver's seat.

He had seen the overturned quad bike from the top of the hill seconds before he saw Gabby. In those seconds he had lived the nightmare that haunted his dreams. For a terrible moment he could feel the weight of his daughter's lifeless body in his arms the same way he had felt her mother's—it was his job to keep her safe and he had failed.

Then he saw her, recognised even at a distance the familiar defiant stance, and the guilt and grief were replaced by immense relief, which in its turn was seamlessly swallowed up by a wave of savage anger. An anger that quickly shifted focus when he identified the tall blonde-haired figure beside his daughter.

He should have known that she would be involved!

He approached with long angry strides, looking like some sort of avenging dark angel—the fallen variety. Lucy didn't blame the kid for looking terrified. She gave the shaking child's shoulder a comforting squeeze. Really, she should have guessed when the child had started talking casually about helicopters, but she hadn't. For some reason she hadn't thought about Santiago Silva as married, let alone a widow, or a father! It was still a struggle to think of him as any of these things, as was maintaining her smile as he approached.

Yesterday she had been conscious that where this man was concerned the veneer of civilisation was pretty thin; right now it was non-existent. He was scary but also, she admitted as she felt a little shiver trace a path down her rigid spine, pretty magnificent!

He swept straight past her, but not before Lucy had felt the icy blast of the glittering stare that dashed over her face.

She watched as he placed his hands on his daughter's shoulders and squatted until he was at face level with her.

'Gabby, you...' Torn between a desire to throttle his wilful daughter and crush her in a bear hug, he took a deep breath. Feeling like a hopelessly inadequate parent, he searched her face and asked brusquely, 'You are hurt?'

Even Lucy, who was extremely unwilling to assign any normal human emotions to this awful man, could not deny the rough concern in his deep voice was genuine.

'I'm fine, *Papá*. She—' the little girl cast a smile in Lucy's direction '—helped me.'

'Not really.'

For a moment his burning eyes met hers, then, a muscle along his clean shaven jaw clenching, he turned away, rising to his feet with a graceful fluidity that caused Lucy's over-sensitive stomach to flip.

'Papá...'

'Wait in the car, Gabriella.'

With one last look over her shoulder at Lucy, she walked, head down, towards the car.

Without looking to see if his daughter had obeyed, Santiago Silva began to speak into the phone he had pulled from the breast pocket of his open necked shirt.

Lucy's Spanish was good enough to make out that the conversation was with a doctor who was being requested to meet them at the *castillo*.

He might be an awful man but he was also obviously a concerned father. 'She wasn't unconscious or anything.'

Santiago closed the phone with a click and covered the space between them in two strides.

As he bent his face close to her own Lucy felt the full force of his contempt as he responded in a lethally soft voice,

'When I require your medical expertise I will ask for it. As for having any contact with my daughter...' He swallowed, the muscles in his brown throat visibly rippling. 'Do not attempt to make any contact or you will be sorry.'

Lucy's sympathy vanished and her anger rushed in to fill the vacuum it left. She didn't bother asking if that had been a threat—it clearly was.

Fighting the urge to step back, she lifted her chin to a pugnacious angle and enquired coolly, 'So, the next time I find her trapped under a grown-up toy she is clearly not old enough to get behind the wheel of, I'll walk by on the other side of the damned road, shall I, Mr Silva? That might be your style, but it isn't mine.'

'I know all about your *style* and I would prefer that members of my family are not contaminated by your toxic influence...but, yes, you did try and help my daughter, so thank you for that at least.'

It was clear that every word of the apology hurt him. 'Does it occur to you that your daughter wouldn't feel the need to break the rules if you cut her a bit of slack?'

He stared at her incredulously. 'You are giving me advice on parenting? So, how many children do you have, Miss Fitzgerald?'

She sucked in a furious breath. Where did this man get off being so superior? 'Well, if I did have one I'd make damned sure I wasn't too busy to notice she had driven off on a quad bike!'

The expression that Lucy saw move at the back of his eyes—so bleak it was almost haunted—made her almost regret her taunt, but she stifled the stab of guilt. She'd save her pity for someone who deserved it. He was a bully, used to people sitting and taking what he dished out.

Well, she wasn't going to take it, not from him, not from anyone.

'Stay away from my family or I will make you wish you'd never been born.' Without waiting for her response, he turned and started walking towards the car.

By the time she reached the *finca* Lucy was so mad she was shaking like someone with a fever.

'Lucy, my dear, what's wrong? What's happened?' Harriet studied the face of her ex-student with growing concern.

'Nothing, I'm fine. Don't get up,' she added as the older woman struggled to rise from her chair. 'You should have rested longer. You know what the doctor said about keeping your foot up to stop it swelling again.'

Harriet subsided back into her seat with a frustrated grunt. 'I'll stay here if you tell me what's wrong, Lucy.'

In the middle of pacing agitatedly across the room, Lucy paused, her fists in tight balls at her sides, her face coloured by two bright spots of anger on her smooth cheeks, and gave a high little laugh. 'Mr Smug Sanctimonious Creep Silva is wrong!'

Harriet looked confused. 'Ramon!' she exclaimed. 'But he seems a sweet boy, if a little full of himself...whatever has he done?' She had never seen the student she considered one of the brightest young women she had ever taught lose her air of serene calm. Even during the awful press witch hunt she had remained cool and aloof.

'Ramon...?' Lucy shook her head impatiently and took up her pacing. 'It's not Ramon, it's his brother,' she gritted.

'Santiago? You've met him...is he here?'

Lucy gave a grim smile. 'Oh, yes, I've had that pleasure twice now.' She reached for the phone and punched in the number she had scribbled down on the pad beside it. 'Ramon...?' Lucy slowed her agitated breathing and took a deep breath. 'Dinner tonight...?'

When she told Harriet the full story her old tutor was

sympathetic but, to her annoyance, inclined to make excuses for Santiago Silva. 'He jumped to conclusions and
that was wrong.'

'He virtually called me a tart and now today he flings
out his threats!' Lucy raged. Even thinking about the man
made her want to smash things. Nobody had ever got under
her skin this way.

'Why not let me explain the situation to him, Lucy?'

Lucy's lower lip jutted mutinously. 'Why should I explain?
He's the one in the wrong.'

'Gabby is the apple of his eye and very wilful. He's also
very protective of his younger brother. I understand their
father died when Ramon was just a boy, and Santiago was
very young when he inherited the *estancia*. Reading between
the lines, I get the impression that given half the chance his
stepmother fancied herself as the power behind the throne,
so to speak, which from what I know of her would have been
a disaster,' Harriet confided. 'Santiago had to establish his
authority from day one. Not easy for a young man, which
might have made him a little—'

'Full of himself?' Lucy suggested acidly. 'The man needs
teaching a lesson.' And *not*, in her opinion, people to make
excuses for him just because he was rich and lived in some
sort of castle.

'Oh, dear! You will be careful, won't you, Lucy? I've
heard reports that suggested Santiago can be ruthless. I'd
not given much credence to them, since successful men tend
to engender jealousy and his reputation here is...well, I've
never heard anyone have a bad word to say. Yet given what
you've said...?'

Lucy smiled. 'I'll be fine.'

CHAPTER THREE

DESPITE the fact she had been a successful model, Lucy had never been obsessed by fashion. This was not to say she didn't like clothes. Her lifestyle now meant comfort was the order of the day; heels were not much good when you were mucking out the stables! However, there were occasions when she got tired of her androgynous work clothes and sensible shoes and then she'd open the wardrobe and spend an hour or so parading around her bedroom in some of the clothes she had kept from her previous life.

It wasn't so much that she missed being a clothes horse, because she didn't; it was more she missed being, well...a woman!

And now, feeling the silky swish of a dress that had come from the designer in question's famous 'Marilyn Collection'—a gift, he'd said, because she had made him wish he were straight—Lucy had to admit the bright red dress really did do some amazing things for her figure, making her waist look tiny and her curves look lush.

She brushed her hands down the bodice and glanced in the mirror. The figure-hugging cut made the fabric cling to the long lines of her thighs when she moved. The effect was sexy and provocative, which seemed appropriate when what she wanted to do was provoke! Her anger felt strange when she'd spent the last four years trying to play down her looks and blend in.

An image of Santiago Silva's autocratic dark features formed in her head and the beginnings of doubt faded. Pursing her lips, Lucy gave her reflection a nod. The look was exactly what she wanted. Now, she told herself, was not the time for doubts.

'Wow, you look…' Ramon swallowed '…different.'

She arched a brow and, closing the door, followed him across the yard. 'Different good or different bad?' she teased.

Ramon laughed and opened the door to his low-slung car. 'Oh, definitely good, but it's lucky you didn't look like that the first time I saw you.'

'Why?' Lucy was curious.

'Because I wouldn't have dared approach you. You look way out of my league tonight, Lucy.'

'I'm still me.' Lucy felt uneasy, Ramon's appreciation bordering on reverence.

The sense of anticipation and righteous indignation she had begun the journey with began to fade by the time they reached the massive gates of the Silva *estancia*, replaced by a growing sense of unease and guilt.

What the hell was she doing? This was a crazy idea! She glanced towards Ramon and thought, *Not just crazy—cruel.* In her determination to score points off the awful brother she had not paused to consider the consequences of her actions. Not for one second had she considered the hurt she might be inflicting on the nice brother.

The sense of shame grew until she couldn't bear it another second.

'I can't,' she muttered under her breath as she reached for her seat belt. 'Stop!'

Ramon responded to the shrill screech and hit the brake,

jerking Lucy, who had freed herself from the belt, into the windscreen.

'*Madre mia*, are you all right?'

Lucy rubbed her head and leaned back in the seat. 'Fine,' she said, dismissing his concern with a shake of her head and then regretting it, she had the start of a headache.

'What's wrong?' Ramon cast a questioning look at her tense profile. 'I could have slowed down, all you had to do was ask,' he joked lightly as he wound down the window. 'That was quite a bang you took.'

'It's nothing.'

'So, other than my driving, what's the problem?'

Lucy looked at Ramon and read concern in his handsome face. She bit her lip, feeling more guilty than ever. She took a deep breath. There was no way she could continue with the charade so it was best to come clean now.

'No, I'm not all right—I'm a total bitch!' Not as much of a bitch as Santiago Silva thought she was, but it was a close thing.

Ramon looked annoyingly unconvinced by her emotional claim.

'When I rang you it wasn't…it was a mistake. I'm sorry. I know I let you believe, but the—I'm not interested in you that way…'

Ramon did not display the shock she had anticipated. 'I did wonder… So, you don't fancy me?'

She flashed him a grateful look and shook her head slowly. 'I really am sorry.'

'Are you sure you don't fancy me?'

This drew a laugh from Lucy, who begged, 'Please don't be nice to me! I feel awful enough as it is.'

'Relax, I'll survive. It's not as though I haven't been knocked back before…' He paused and grinned. 'Actually I haven't. I'm wondering why…?'

She shook her head.

As Ramon sat there looking at her in silence for the first time she saw some family resemblance, a likeness to his brother, not so much in the individual features, more the tilt of his head and his hairline…hairline! She frowned. She had only met him the once and the encounter had lasted minutes but weirdly the details of Santiago Silva's face were burned into her brain.

'So why did you ring me and say you'd changed your mind?'

'I was angry and I wanted to punish…'

'Me?'

'No, of course not. The thing is I met your brother and he—he made me mad.'

'Santiago made you mad…?' Ramon echoed in astonishment.

Ramon saw the anger in her sparkling expressive eyes before she tipped her head tightly. 'Yes.' He grew curious. This was not the usual impression his brother made on women.

'When did you meet Santiago? What did he do?'

Lucy rolled down her window and took a gulp of fresh night air redolent of pine. 'I met him yesterday and then again this morning…' For a split second she considered telling him the truth, but held back. What was it about that wretched man that turned her into some sort of petty vengeful cow?

It wasn't as if people had not thought and said worse about her. Why had his assumption got to her this way? Just thinking about him made her skin prickle.

'It…it was something and nothing, really,' she admitted, rubbing her arms as if she could rub away the memory. 'He recognised me yesterday. You don't know, but a few years ago I—'

'Oh, the super-injunction stuff, you mean.'

Lucy stared at him in astonishment. 'You know about that?'

Ramon, who was adjusting his tie in the rear-view mirror, turned his head and looked amused. 'Of course I know about it, Lucy.'

'But how?'

He waved his mobile phone at her. 'I punched in your name, though actually,' he admitted, 'I was checking out your age on the off chance...not that I have a problem with an older woman,' he added quickly. 'In fact, but well, never mind. Imagine my surprise when I got not only your age but the other stuff, too.'

'Oh!' Lucy said, feeling foolish for not anticipating this possibility. It was impossible to have secrets when all someone had to do was punch in a name and your life—or a version of it—appeared on a screen.

'So all this...' the expressive downward sweep of his hand took in the silk that clung like a second skin to her body '...is for Santiago's benefit, not mine.'

His brother sounded more philosophical than annoyed by this discovery, but Lucy was horrified by the suggestion.

'Of course not!' She almost bounced in her seat in her enthusiasm to deny the suggestion. Then as she examined her conscience she added, 'Well, not in that way.'

'So what did big brother do to make you so mad? Threaten to have you arrested for corrupting a minor? Have you framed for a felony? Pay you to leave the country?'

Lucy looked away quickly, but not quickly enough.

Ramon's joking expression vanished. '*Dio*, he did, didn't he? Santiago tried to pay you off?'

'He...sort of,' she admitted, feeling reluctant to tell tales.

'I don't believe it,' Ramon breathed, looking stunned.

'I understand your brother wanted to protect you. It's only

natural.' She stopped and thought, *Why am I defending the man who is clearly a total control freak?*

'Will you do me a favour, Lucy?'

Lucy quashed her instinct to say anything out of sympathy. 'That depends,' she responded warily.

'Go through with your plan to teach my big brother a lesson.'

For the first time Lucy heard anger in his voice and realised that it was aimed, not at her, but his brother.

'I'm sure he thought he was doing the right thing…'

'You're still defending him?'

'No, of course I'm not,' she replied indignantly. 'I think your brother is the most…' She became aware of Ramon's expression and stopped.

'He's really got under your skin, hasn't he?' he observed.

Lucy adopted an amused expression and lied. 'It takes more than your brother to get under my skin.'

'You won't deny that he needs teaching a lesson…?' She nodded—how could she not? 'So why not give him a night to remember? Why not? You're all dressed up and nowhere to go. Please…for me?' he coaxed. 'Or if not, for good old-fashioned revenge? I'm tired of Santiago always thinking he knows what is best for me. For once, I'd like him to treat me like a man. I know he means it for the best and I know my mother gives him a hard time and blames him every time I mess up, but it's humiliating and…'

'You want to teach him a lesson.'

Ramon nodded. 'He's gone too far this time and he's involved a friend. What'll he do the next time—lock me in my room? I'd just like to be the one doing the manipulating for once, so he knows what it feels like.'

Lucy sighed. 'I'm probably going to regret this…'

* * *

'My God, it's a castle.' Lucy sat awestruck in her seat as Ramon stood by the open door. 'Enormous!' she breathed, staring at the intimidating edifice lit by strategically placed spotlights. 'As in national monument enormous…is that tower Moorish?'

Ramon cast a negligent look over his shoulder. 'I think… yeah, it's big,' he agreed.

She started to shake her head. 'I can't do this.'

Ramon grabbed her arm and hauled her out. 'No, you're not going to chicken out now. It was your idea, remember.'

The impetus of his tug made her stagger into his arms. 'A terrible idea!' she muttered in his ear, drawing a laugh from Ramon.

'Are you not going to introduce me to your guest?'

The voice as smooth as silk made the hairs on the back of her neck stand on end. The only thing that prevented her jumping away from Ramon was the hand in the small of her back.

'Of course.'

Ramon loosed her but as she pulled away grabbed her hand.

Lucy took a deep breath, the surface of her skin prickling in a weird response to the sound of his voice. 'Good evening.' She turned her head as Santiago Silva emerged fully from the shadows.

Her already rapid heart picked up tempo as she struggled to hide her reaction, not that he could be unaccustomed to attracting awed stares.

He was, she admitted, pretty awesome and she was staring.

She struggled to direct her gaze past him, but like a compass point returning north her eyes zeroed back to the tall, rampantly male figure dressed in a beautifully cut dark suit teamed with a white shirt he wore open at the neck. The informality went skin deep; he looked exclusively and every inch the autocratic patrician occupier of a castle.

He inclined his dark head, the courtesy of the gesture doing nothing to disguise the predatory gleam in his hooded eyes.

She was no adrenaline junkie but she imagined it might feel this way to jump out of a plane with nothing but a parachute. Actually maybe not even the parachute, she thought, moistening her dry lips with the tip of her tongue.

The nervous action drew his dark gaze to her mouth.

Lucy swallowed and felt a flicker of apprehension. Harriet had warned her that this was not a man to be messed with and she was messing. Was she mad or just…? She swallowed, suddenly identifying the emotion mingled in with the trepidation as *excitement*… Yes, clearly she was mad!

Santiago recognised the surge of molten anger he felt as he watched them, but refused to acknowledge the accompanying emotion as being related in any way to jealousy. He was not jealous of his brother; he was furious! Furious that Ramon could be so stupid; frustrated that he could not think above waist level; that he could not see past the stunning beauty of the woman in his arms.

He, on the other hand, could compartmentalise, think past the painful level of his arousal. She really was the embodiment of sin, he decided, swallowing hard as his burning glance moved over the undulating curves of her body. She was sheathed in a tight red dress that would probably and legitimately in his opinion be illegal in several countries.

'Lucy, this is my big brother, Santiago…Santiago, this is Lucy.'

Ramon pushed her forward with a pat on her bottom that under other circumstances Lucy would have objected to, and she found herself taking a stumbling step towards Santiago. Recovering her poise and covering her growing anxiety behind a plastic smile, she took a second, more graceful step, murmuring a good evening and ignoring the voice in her head that was counselling she run in the opposite direction.

Her half-extended hand fell away as Santiago met her midway. Bending down towards her—not something that happened a lot when you were five ten in your bare feet— he planted his hands on her shoulders.

The light touch concealed a strength that she felt as strongly as the brush of his breath on her cheek. Steeling herself for an air kiss, she stiffened, gasped faintly and closed her eyes as his mouth, his lips, lightly touched her skin.

Feeling the responsive quiver run through her body, he smiled and bent in closer.

'Great work,' he admired. 'Though you might want to rethink the dress—it's a bit obvious—but the husky sexy voice, nice touch, I like it...'

The blue eyes winked wider in protest. 'What? Husky, sexy? I wasn't...'

She stopped, remembering just in time her role of heartless courtesan, and produced a wide, brilliantly insincere smile as she whispered back, 'In my experience—'

'No doubt vast.' His nostrils quivered in response to the fragrance she wore. It smelt of something light, floral and very feminine.

'You have no idea.' A joking comment made by her solicitor drifted back into her head. 'The only way we can legally clear your name is to produce a medical certificate saying you're a virgin.' He had never appreciated the black irony. 'In my experience there is no such thing as too obvious when it comes to men, and if you think that was sexy... watch and learn...'

She let her voice trail away significantly and had the satisfaction of seeing a muscle along his hard jaw clench. She lifted her chin, turning a deaf ear to the voice in her head that was screaming warnings about playing with fire. Instead of lowering the temperature she raised it several degrees, responding to the anger she saw reflected back at her in the dark surface of his eyes with a slow 'cat got the cream' smile.

The guiding hand that then slid to her elbow was not this time light, but she refused to give him the satisfaction of reacting to the biting, bone-crushing grip of his fingers. With Ramon walking on the other side of her, he steered her towards the sweep of stairs that led to the massive porticoed entrance.

Feeling more frogmarched than guided, she lifted the ankle-length hem of her skirt as gracefully as she could and took the first step up.

It's never too late to run.

CHAPTER FOUR

THE door pushed wider and a figure appeared at the top of the stairs. For a moment Lucy thought it was a child, then as she stepped into a shaft of light thrown by one of the spotlights that illuminated the building Lucy realised it was actually a young woman.

She was petite and wand slim, her slender curves almost hidden by the long black fine-knit silk sweater teamed with black leggings she wore. Not a look many could have pulled off, but this girl did!

Ramon, with an exclamation of welcome, pushed past Lucy. 'Carmella!'

As she watched the two embrace Lucy was very aware of dark eyes watching her like the hawk Santiago reminded her of—it wasn't just the nose and the hauteur, but the predatory ruthlessness. She schooled her expression into serene neutrality and considered the situation objectively—or as objectively as was possible when your body was humming with an uncomfortable combination of antagonism and a heart-pounding awareness that made her skin prickle. The wretched man set every nerve ending in her body on edge. She longed to put some distance between herself and the weird electrical charge-negative he exuded. God, even her scalp was tingling!

Presumably the presence of the tiny creature with the

slow dark eyes and slender graceful body had been invited as the competition. She was definitely a dramatic contrast, the more so because the young woman wore flat leather pumps as opposed to Lucy's four-inch spiky heels!

Coming level with the younger woman, Lucy immediately felt big, blowsy and clumsy next to this delicate creature who emerged from Ramon's embrace looking flustered.

'Lucy, this is Carmella—she's like the little sister I never had. What are you doing here, Melly?'

The girl looked towards Santiago, who said smoothly, 'Does there have to be a reason?'

Conscious of the hand on her elbow, Lucy performed the move she had been mentally rehearsing. It went flawlessly. 'Oh, I'm so sorry.' She tossed a look of sparkling insincerity up at the man whose foot she had just ground with four inches of spiky heel. It had to have hurt, but other than a grunt of shocked pain he had sucked it up like a real tough guy.

Santiago acknowledged her apology with a slight tip of his dark head and a white wolfish grin that carried a promise of retribution.

Conscious of a fizz of excitement in place of the more appropriate trepidation, Lucy lowered her gaze.

'I'm so clumsy,' she trilled.

Clumsy! A laugh locked in the back of his throat, Santiago sucked in a sharp breath through flared nostrils. The last thing in the world anyone would use to describe this woman would be *clumsy*. Her every move was imbued with a sinuous, sensual, seductive grace. Yes, she might represent everything he loathed and despised, but even with the overkill of hip swinging she was the epitome of grace.

After a struggle Lucy broke her gaze free of his dark, compelling, almost hypnotic stare and, reckless excitement still humming through her body, turned with a smile to the girl.

'Hello, Carmella.' From the way the little brunette was looking at Ramon it seemed doubtful that she felt very sisterly towards him. Poor girl, she was clearly crazy about Ramon and his brother could not be unaware of the fact, yet it hadn't stopped him using her to provide a distraction. He obviously didn't care whose feelings he trampled so long as he got what he wanted. Lucy's blood boiled when she thought of all the casualties he must have left in his wake.

Ramon was right: it was about time someone gave him a taste of his own medicine.

'Carmella is a ballet dancer,' Ramon said, switching to English as the two broke off their conversation.

'Back row of the corps de ballet,' the girl corrected, looking embarrassed by the accolade.

The conversation had taken them through a hallway of epic cavernous proportions. This place was not what anyone would term cosy, but it was impressive. Had the circumstances been different she would have been bombarding her host with questions about the history of this fantastic building.

'How interesting,' she said, meaning it. She had had ballet classes herself until it became obvious that she was not built on the right scale.

Santiago, who had been speaking in a softly spoken aside to a dark-suited individual who had silently materialised, murmured, 'Thank you, Josef,' before turning back to them. 'It appears our meal is ready. So, what do you do, Lucy?'

Caught off guard by the addition, Lucy blinked. It took her a second to recover her poise and resist the compulsion to say, 'Live off impressionable boys.' Lucy didn't know how she managed to suppress the words hovering on the tip of her tongue.

'I manage to keep busy.'

'And you're staying at the resort hotel? I just love the spa there,' Carmella enthused.

'Isn't that where you usually get your dinner dates, Ramon?' Lucy teased, forgetting for one moment her role. 'Actually, I'm staying with a friend.' She broke off and swallowed a gasp. The room they had entered had the dimensions of a baronial hall complete with tapestries that were probably priceless on the stone walls; all that was missing was someone playing a lute in the minstrels' gallery. The candles on the table, heavy with silver and gleaming crystal, had been lit. A person would need a megaphone to speak to a person sitting at the far end of the table.

'How…cosy,' she murmured sarcastically.

'Friend?' Santiago angled his question towards his brother, not Lucy, pulling out a chair for Lucy at the table and ensuring that several feet of antique oak separated her from Ramon. Not that he would have been surprised if the woman had slithered across the surface to latch onto her prey.

An image flashed into his head of her lying across the table in a silvery pool of her own hair, the slinky red dress pulled up to reveal her long legs, one arm lifted in supplication. He froze the frame before it progressed and deleted it, but not before his temperature had risen by several degrees.

Three pairs of eyes swivelled his way as he cleared his throat; he turned his head sharply to block out the blue. 'What friend?'

'Harriet Harris,' Ramon supplied.

His brother's expression was openly sceptical as he turned to Lucy, looking at her accusingly from dark brows that had formed an interrogative straight line.

'The Cambridge don…?'

She would have been amused by the proof of his snobbish prejudice had her normally lively sense of humour survived the trauma of the evening.

'Yes, that's right,' she said, thinking, *Sorry for stepping out of the box you've put me into.* Her scorn increased. Presumably in his world she and women like Harriet occupied separate universes.

'How do you come to know Harriet Harris?'

'She was my personal tutor when I was at Cambridge.'

She had the satisfaction of seeing shock he could not conceal chase across his lean features. 'You were a Cambridge student?'

She nodded, still smiling, counted to ten, but she was unable to hide the growing antagonism that revealed itself in the sparkle in her electric-blue eyes.

'You graduated?'

He sounded as though discovering that Martians had landed was a lot more probable. At that moment Lucy, who habitually played down her intellect—bad enough being head and shoulders above your contemporaries at school without being a swot—would have happily shoved her certificates down his throat if she had them to hand.

Ramon saved her from replying to this continued interrogation. 'She came to the rescue to help Harriet.'

'To the rescue once again,' he drawled, drawing a puzzled look from his brother. 'From what does Harriet need rescuing?' The local community had initially been wary of the Englishwoman who had moved here two years ago. She was still considered eccentric for her alarming multicoloured hair and her devotion to the donkeys she provided a sanctuary for, but she had endeared herself by learning the language and integrating with the local community.

'She's broken her leg.'

'Dios!' he exclaimed, displaying what, had it been anyone else, Lucy would have considered concern. In his case she attributed his reaction to a pathological need to be in

charge. The man was a total control freak. 'Why did I not
know of this?'

Yes, a control freak of epic proportions!

'And why did Anton not inform me?'

Lucy didn't have a clue who Anton was but he had her
sympathy. God, working for Santiago Silva would be like
working for some feudal warlord... Of course, a very good-
looking feudal warlord, she conceded, her eyes drifting over
the length of his long greyhound-sleek, lean, hard body and
one with very good hygiene—the scent of the cologne he
used mingled with warm male showed a tendency to linger in
her nostrils. She gave her head a tiny shake and looked away.

'Is she in hospital?'

His manager dealt with the everyday burden of the estate but Santiago was not an anonymous landlord. He made
it his business to know all his tenants and took an active interest in the village, just as his father had done. He took the
responsibility that came with his role here seriously and he
got a lot from it.

When you worked in finance it was easy to lose sight of
the human face behind the columns of clinical figures, but
here he saw firsthand how decisions made in a boardroom
could affect people's lives. This was not to say he didn't get
a buzz from what he did, but the estate and the people who
lived and worked on it kept him grounded.

Duty might be an unfashionable word but it was deeply
ingrained in Santiago. Even so, the early days had not been
easy. When still grieving for his father he had found himself
expected to step into his shoes—and they were big shoes to
fill. He'd been living with Magdalena in the city when his
father died. She had been really supportive and it had seemed
natural to ask her to move with him to the *castillo*. He had
not anticipated she would take the request for a marriage
proposal but after the initial shock he had thought why not?

It would happen eventually. Now he recognised that it might very well not have happened, that had things been different they would have eventually drifted apart.

'Only for a day. She's at home now. And don't blame Anton—when he left for his cousin's wedding I think maybe I told him I'd tell you when you got back,' Ramon admitted with a rueful grin.

One sable brow lifted. 'Maybe?'

'All right, I said I would, but no harm done,' he added cheerfully. 'Lucy is helping Harriet until she gets back on her feet.'

Santiago's glance slid from his brother to the woman sitting to his left. Was Ramon joking? Did his brother seriously think this woman would do anything that risked chipping her nail varnish? His glance slid automatically to the hand that held the goblet, though she appeared not to have touched the wine it held.

His sneer faded as he registered the fingers curved lightly around the stem. They were long and shapely but the pearly nails were neither long nor painted; they were trimmed short and unvarnished. With a tiny shake of his head he dismissed the incongruity. Short nails did not make her any the less useless when it came to manual labour, and donkeys might be appealing to look at, but they were high-maintenance animals, not to mention deserving of their stubborn reputation.

'She couldn't be in better hands,' Ramon continued.

The words brought an image of his half-brother enjoying the ministrations of those hands, except it wasn't his brother he was seeing... Santiago stiffened. 'I doubt very much if Miss Fitzgerald—'

'Oh, that's so formal. Please call me Lucy.' Maintaining the saccharine sweet smile was making her facial muscles ache.

Santiago, who could think of several things he'd like to call her, smiled back.

As their eyes connected black on bright cornflower-blue, clashed and remained sealed Lucy was seized by a determination not to be, on principle, the first one to look away. The effort of following through with her childish self-imposed endurance race brought a faint sheen of moisture to her skin. In the distance she was vaguely aware of Ramon and Carmella's voices as they laughed and chatted, the sound softer than the sound of the blood that pounded in her ears.

On the other side of the table Ramon knocked over a glass. The sound as the crystal hit the floor was like a pistol shot. It was hard to say which one of them looked away first but all that mattered to Lucy was that the accident had splintered the growing tension. A silent sigh left her parted lips as Lucy squeezed her eyes closed, just glad that she had broken that nerve-shredding contact.

'Speak English…' She heard Santiago reproach the young couple who were exchanging laughing comments in Spanish. 'Lucy will be feeling excluded.'

As if that wasn't the idea, Lucy thought, opening her eyes and switching to her less than perfect Spanish as she said, 'No problem. I need the practice.'

She saw a spasm of annoyance move across his face as he turned his accusing stare her way. 'You speak Spanish?'

Assuming his irritation stemmed from the fact blonde trollops in his world were not allowed to speak any language but avarice, she chose to reply in English.

'A little.'

'More than a little. She also speaks French, Italian, German, and…Gaelic…?' inserted Ramon from across the table.

Lucy nodded, impressed that he had remembered.

'Not just a pretty face and perfect body…' he added, with his eyes trained on her bosom. 'She has brains, too… Do I know how to pick them or do I know how to pick them?'

He smiled sunnily at his brother, inviting his admiration before rising from his chair to give access to the maid who had come to remove the broken glass.

'Quite the linguist.'

'My family is quite...cosmopolitan.' A massive understatement—the Fitzgerald clan was spread across the globe. 'Actually Ramon is being kind. My Spanish really is pretty basic,' she admitted in a burst of honesty, forgetting for a moment that her character did not do self-deprecating or honest.

She almost immediately retrieved the situation and invited his anger by dropping her voice a sexy octave. 'I'm hoping to improve my vocabulary considerably during my stay.' She produced a close approximation of the look she had used to sell everything from shampoo to insurance as she looked at Ramon from under the sweep of her fluttering lashes, feeling just as silly now as she had back then when the photographers had asked her to smoulder.

'And Ramon is such a good teacher.'

It wasn't just the open provocation, it was the fact that he was not immune to the effects of her husky purr that fanned his smouldering anger into full-blown flames.

Her glance swivelled sideways in response to the sound of a cut-glass goblet coming down with a crash on the table. Catching the edge of Santiago's thunderous glare, she thought, *You haven't lost it, Lucy.*

'So are you, *querida*.' Across the table Ramon picked up the cue, fixed his eyes on her bosom and added throatily, 'I'm learning a lot from you.'

For a moment Lucy was in danger of slipping out of character. She bit her quivering lower lip and brought her eyelids down to hide the laughter sparkling in her eyes. Ramon was getting into his role a little too enthusiastically. If he didn't watch himself his brother was going to smell a rat. She somehow doubted he'd see the funny side.

Was there a funny side?

She reached for her glass and drained the contents. If anyone noticed her burning cheeks she could blame the alcohol, for heartless seductresses did not blush.

'It's always a pleasure to teach a willing pupil.'

Worried that this might be over the top, too, she slid a surreptitious glance towards the man sitting beside her. He was totally still…still as in 'a volcano about to explode' still. She needn't have worried, he seemed only too happy to believe she was a total trollop.

'So do you have a big family, Lucy?'

Lucy smiled. Carmella seemed blissfully ignorant of the undercurrents swirling around the table. 'Vast. I have nine siblings—my father had three wives.' Her own mother was his last.

'Presumably not all at once.'

Lucy clenched her teeth and bridled at the amused contempt in Santiago's voice. The man was the most smug, self-satisfied creep she had ever met. Plan or no plan, while she was willing to stomach his insults and digs when she was the target she would not tolerate him insulting her family, who had rallied around protectively when she'd needed them.

It was true that when he was alive Lucy had had her share of disagreements with her father, culminating in the massive argument that had ended with her leaving home rather than follow the course in life he had chosen for her.

Determined to show she could make it alone, Lucy had started modelling, her intention being to make enough to fund her degree. She hadn't anticipated for one moment that she would have the sort of incredible success she had enjoyed…though actually the world of modelling had never been one she enjoyed, however much she'd loved the freedom making that sort of money gave her.

It still did. Her father had been right about one thing—she

had inherited his financial acumen, though not the buzz he spoke of that came when you had nailed a deal. The investments she had made at the time had weathered the global downturn and enabled her to live comfortably off the income.

The thing that mattered was that when she had needed him her dad had been there, as had all her family, and she wasn't about to sit by and let this man look down his nose at them.

'And do you share your father's attitude to marriage?'

'According to my mother I'm very like him.' She shrugged and, dropping her role of seductress, added with quiet dignity, 'I can't see it myself, but I really hope I share both my parents' values.'

Did he look taken aback by her reply? It would seem she had imagined it because when he replied it was with that now familiar nasty smile that made her fingers itch with an uncharacteristic desire to slap his smug face.

'I'm sure they are both proud of you.'

Clearly there was more to Lucy Fitzgerald than met the eye. He'd been so confident removing her from Ramon's life would be easy that he hadn't even bothered spending five minutes researching the details of the scandal—a fundamental error. His mistake was that he'd been treating this problem differently from those he encountered in his business dealings—he'd made the error of letting it become personal.

If she had weaknesses beyond greed, he would discover them, though of course it was inevitable that greed would be her downfall.

He suddenly saw the headline under a photo of her shielding her eyes from flashes as a man helped her into a blacked-out limo, and experienced a eureka moment.

'Your father is Patrick Fitzgerald!'

The accusation drew a grunt of amazement from Ramon, who forgot his besotted act as he stared at his brother. 'You didn't know?' He suddenly grinned and taunted, 'I thought you knew everything.'

'Who is Patrick Fitzgerald?' Carmella asked.

Ramon laughed. 'Melly doesn't read books, do you, angel? Just celebrity magazines.'

The girl kicked him under the table and he laughed, snatching away her plate that held a bread roll, teasing, 'Careful, you might put on an ounce looking at it. Seriously, Lucy's dad had a finger in many pies—he was a bit of a legend actually—but he was about the most powerful publisher on the planet... He was—' He glanced towards Lucy.

'My dad died last year,' she explained to Carmella. 'He'd been retired for a while.'

Santiago continued to feel annoyed with himself for not making the connection sooner. He had not met the man, but Ramon was right—in financial circles he had been pretty much a legend, a man who had started the publishing house that had become the biggest and most successful in the world and still remained in the hands of the same family today.

He felt an unexpected stab of sympathy for Fitzgerald, who had been known to guard his privacy jealously. It must have been hell for him to see his daughter publicly humiliated and her sordid secrets shared with the world, and of course it was always the parents' fault—a universally accepted premise that every parent was conscious of.

Santiago had lost count of the sleepless nights he had spent second-guessing his parenting decisions and Gabriella was not even in her teens yet. As a man who could afford to indulge his own child, Santiago knew only too well the pitfalls that were out there for a father who did not want his love of his child to ruin her.

If the results were anything to go by, Patrick Fitzgerald had fallen into every pitfall there was. If the man had still been around he might have rung him to ask him how he brought up his daughter so that he could do the exact opposite.

God knew what motivated a woman like Lucy Fitzgerald, but apparently it wasn't money after all. His eyes drifted in her direction just as the maid who had been making a discreet exit with her dustpan paused by Lucy's chair.

'Oh, I am so sorry, miss...your lovely dress. I'll...'

Lucy glanced without interest at the splash of blood stains on her dress and rose to her feet. 'Forget the dress—your hand!' She removed the dustpan from the girl's hand, put it down on her seat and took the injured hand in her own. 'Your poor hand.'

She grabbed a clean napkin from the table and pressed it to the small laceration still oozing a little blood on the girl's palm.

'No, miss, I'm fine, just clumsy.'

'You're not fine...'

Santiago found himself the focus of an accusing icy blue stare that could not have been more condemning had he taken a knife and cut the girl himself.

'It must have hurt like mad and she didn't say a word.' The girl's silence was obviously a symptom of an atmosphere of oppression in the workplace, she decided.

She turned back to the girl, the frost in her eyes warming to concern. 'Look...sorry, I don't know your name?'

'Sabina.'

'Well, Sabina, I think your hand needs cleaning—there might be some shreds of glass in it—and it needs dressing.'

The girl looked confused and Lucy turned to her fellow diners with an expression of exasperation. 'Will someone help me out here?' Her Spanish did not stretch to a translation.

It was Santiago who reacted first. Pushing aside his chair, he moved across to the timid-looking maid and spoke to her in Spanish. Lucy listened, unable to follow the rapid flow of words, noticing how different his voice sounded when he spoke to the girl, how kind and gentle.

Whatever he said made the girl smile and look less terrified. Across the table Ramon added something that drew a weak laugh from her.

Lucy was still holding the napkin to the wound but the girl was staring with starry-eyed devotion up at Santiago. Lucy bit her lip and looked away. Was there a female on the planet who didn't think he walked on water? She thought, *Am I the only person who sees him for what he is?*

'You can let go now, Miss Fitzgerald.'

Lucy started as the sound of Santiago's deep voice jolted her out of her brooding reverie.

'Josef will take over from here.'

'What? Oh, yes, of course.' She nodded to the sober suited solemn-faced man standing at her side and removed her hand from the makeshift dressing. 'You need to apply pressure.'

'Josef is more than capable, Miss Fitzgerald.' Santiago's dismissive glance swept across her face before he turned back to the girl, his manner changing as he spoke to her softly before she was led from the room by the older man.

'Perhaps you would like to clean up, Miss Fitzgerald?'

She glanced down to hide her hot cheeks, mortified as her body reacted with dramatic tingling awareness to the critical clinical stare directed at the smears of blood on the upper slopes of her breasts.

She could see his point, a little blood could go a long way and the smears did look awful.

'And obviously you will send me a bill for the cleaning.'

Actually he was just realising that nothing about this woman was obvious.

She had had an expensive dress ruined and, obviously, spoilt, self-absorbed materialist that she was, there should have been tantrums. But no, what did she do? Go all Mother Teresa on him! And he'd seen her face—her concern was either genuine or she was the best actress he had ever seen.

So maybe she was not all bad, but her redemption was not his business. Saving his brother was.

For Lucy the faint sneer in his voice was the last straw. She could almost hear the sound of her control snapping as she turned on him, eyes blazing, bosom heaving.

'I can pay my own bills. Do you think I give a damn about the dress? I...' She stopped, horrified to feel the prick of tears behind her eyelids. 'I'll go wash up!' she blurted, making a dash for the door.

CHAPTER FIVE

OUTSIDE the room Lucy had composed herself enough to ask for directions to the bathroom when she was approached by a staff member in the bewildering baronial hallway.

In the decadently appointed bathroom she had been directed to, Lucy stood with her hands under the running water, waiting for the desire to cry her eyes out to subside.

Finally feeling marginally more composed, she looked at her reflection in the mirror above the marble washbasin. The lighting above it emphasised the waxy pallor of her oval face; she didn't even have her bag with her to make running repairs to her make-up.

With a deep troubled sigh she set about sponging the smears of blood from her skin and clothes.

Reluctant to leave the marble lined sanctuary, Lucy stood with her back against the cool wall. She shook her head, still totally bewildered. She had no idea what had been going on in there, didn't have a clue why she had blown up that way.

Her efforts to analyse what had happened and why were hindered by the fact that every time she felt an answer to the puzzle was in reach, the image of his dark face and sleek body rose in her head, effectively blanking everything else.

What is your problem Lucy? He was *meant* to think she cared more about dresses than people, that had been the idea, so why had she reacted that way?

She had no idea how long she had been standing there before there was a tentative tap on the door. It was followed by a voice calling her name.

'I just wondered—are you all right, Lucy?'

Lucy straightened her shoulders, took a deep sustaining breath and opened the door. An anxious-looking Ramon, who was standing directly behind it, took a step back.

'I'm fine,' she said, forcing a smile as she emerged. 'Sorry about that but I've never liked the sight of even a speck of blood.' She stopped and shook her head and looked at him with eyes dark with emotion. 'I'm fine with blood, Ramon, but not your brother. I can't do this...over the years I've developed a thick skin but somehow he manages... I'm tired of being judged,' she finished with a weary sigh.

Ramon shook his head and looked remorseful as he enfolded her in a comforting bear hug. 'God, no, it's me. I shouldn't have asked you to do this. It's my problem, not yours, and to be honest I wasn't expecting Santiago to be quite so...' His hands slid down her arms and stayed there.

Standing in the loose circle of his arms, Lucy gave a shrug. 'And you thought I could take it? I thought so, too,' she admitted. 'I really don't care what your brother thinks of me,' she hastened to assure Ramon. 'But this stopped being my idea of a fun evening when he started making snide remarks about my family.'

'I understand,' Ramon said.

Lucy was wondering a little uneasily about the inflection in his voice when he reached out and touched her forehead. 'God, you're going to have a bruise there,' he said, touching the discoloured area that was developing on her forehead. 'You really took a bang.'

Santiago stood in the minstrels' gallery, his unblinking stare trained on the couple below, tension vibrating in every taut fibre of his lean body as he listened to the buzz of their soft voices, unable to make out the words, but you didn't need words to see the intimacy in the way they stood close together.

When his brother touched her face tenderly he turned, biting back a harsh gasp as he felt something kick hard and low in his belly.

'I'll try and stay in character,' Lucy promised Ramon. 'But after tonight that's it.'

She returned to the dining room with some trepidation, but the rest of meal passed relatively uneventfully. Their host showed little inclination to make conversation other than a few passing asides to Carmella, which should have been a good thing but turned out not to be.

Lucy was painfully conscious of his eyes following her and spent the entire meal waiting for him to pounce, so tense that every bone in her body ached with it.

And of course she did what she always did when she was nervous: she babbled like an idiot until the sound of her own bright chattering voice was giving even her a headache. Afterwards she didn't have a clue what she had been talking about, which was probably a good thing.

Santiago excused himself before coffee was served and Lucy used his absence to make her own hurried exit. Outside, it was a beautiful night. She released a long sigh and breathed in the fresh night air almost dizzy with relief that the ordeal was over.

Just behind her she was conscious of Ramon pausing to speak to the man who had emerged from the house but the effort of translating what they were saying was beyond her.

She was struggling to think anything beyond the fact that she was escaping from this place and that hateful man; she wanted to forget the entire evening had ever happened.

And she would—tomorrow she would go back to doing what she had actually come here to do. God knew why she had ever got involved. It wasn't as if she hadn't been insulted before, but she had never lowered herself to her persecutor's level; she had always maintained her silence and the moral high ground.

Anyway this was not her battle, it was Ramon's. If he had issues with his brother he could sort them out himself.

'Wait in the car.'

Lucy automatically extended a hand to catch the keys he threw her. 'What?'

'Phone call. It's urgent and no one can find Santiago. I'll be back in a minute,' Ramon promised, following the sober-suited man back indoors.

No one knows where he is. She glanced back at the building; golden light spilled from the windows making her think of eyes watching her.

'Seriously paranoid, Lucy.' Her laugh had a hollow sound as she turned her back on the building, unable to shake the feeling that the man they couldn't find was in one of those windows watching her.

She shivered and told herself it was the chill in the evening air. Despite this she did not follow Ramon's suggestion and take shelter in the car. Instead Lucy wandered away from the brooding presence of the sombre fortified house.

She had walked some way across the manicured lawn when she found herself drawn towards the sound of water and discovered, not the pond she had expected, but a river.

She walked out onto the wooden bridge and, leaning her arms on the rail, gazed down into the dark water. Her expression was pensive as her thoughts drifted, the memories of the evening revolving in her head. If not the worst night of her life, it had been right up there.

On the plus side—her brow puckered as she struggled

to come up with one, other than the fact the night was over and if she ever saw Santiago Silva again she would leg it in the opposite direction. She was hanging up her scarlet-woman hat.

Trailing a hand towards the water, she leaned farther over the rail, following a leaf caught on the current, running to the opposite side as it disappeared from view to follow its progress.

Santiago, who had followed her from outside the house, watched as she leaned forward. The lust that lay coiled in his belly morphed into alarm as she leaned so far over the rail that she appeared in danger of toppling in. This woman seemed oddly drawn to water and bridges.

'If you're planning on jumping in don't expect me to leap in and save you.'

Lucy started as if shot, took a hasty step backwards and found herself staring at Santiago. He was looking mean, moody and, if she was honest, totally magnificent in the moonlight.

She took a deep breath and lifted her chin as he stepped onto the bridge.

'Relax, I don't need saving. I'm not on the lookout for a white knight.' Which was just as well as he definitely did not meet the criteria...all that dark brooding stuff made him far more likely to be the bad boy.

'That wasn't an offer.'

'And it so happens I swim like a fish.' She felt no guilt for playing up her ability.

'Just as well, given your affinity for water. I keep finding you knee deep.'

She extended a leg, displaying a dry and slightly muddied shoe. 'I wasn't paddling, but I'm a Pisces so maybe that's it, and I wasn't going to jump.'

'No...?'

'You sound disappointed.'

His grin flashed and faded as his dark glance slid down her body. Lucy was disgusted with herself for being unable to control the flash of heat that engulfed her body. Dear God, all the man had to do was look at her and she started acting like some sort of hormonal teenager.

'If I throw you into the water will you sprout a tail and swim away?' It was true, she did look like a particularly sultry mermaid in that dress with the cloud of silvery hair, a siren capable of luring men to their deaths.

And her intended victim was Ramon. His brother's life might not be in danger but his heart was, and he would save Ramon from this woman's clutches by whatever means possible.

And if money was not a lure he would have to think of something that was…and if it required that he used himself as bait it was a sacrifice he was willing to make.

You're a saint, Santiago, admired the sardonic voice in his head.

Lucy inhaled and straightened her shoulders. Her fingers tightened on the wooden rail, her defiant pose perilously fragile as he walked towards her. It was utterly mystifying how a man as big as him could move so silently, like some big jungle cat stalking his prey.

The analogy sent a shiver sliding down her spine as she watched him approach, the golden-toned skin of his throat and face very dark in contrast to the dazzling white of his shirt.

You didn't have to like the man to be utterly riveted by the way he moved and nobody could fail to be aware—in an objective way—of the aura of raw, earthy sensuality he exuded.

Lucy bit her lip and felt her shaky composure develop a few more cracks as he paused, his hand on the rail, a few feet away from her. She looked at his fingers only inches away from her own and tightened her grip, easing her hand back surreptitiously. She had a nasty feeling that if he touched her even lightly those cracks she was aware of would split wide apart.

'Do I make you nervous, Lucy?' he asked, staring at the blue veined pulse point that was throbbing at the base of her throat.

'You'd like that, wouldn't you?'

When he responded to the breathless accusation with a slow smile that said he knew exactly how his presence made her feel, her heart hammered against her ribs. She found herself hating him more than ever. It was weird but she had never felt this sort of violent animosity towards anyone, not even Denis Mulville, who had made her a hate figure out of sheer spite.

'Do you always lurk like that?' She pressed a hand to her breastbone, hating the fact she still sounded breathless because, yes, he made her nervous...not excited, because that would be stupid.

'I'm not lurking. It is my habit to take a walk before I go to bed.'

'Then don't let me stop you.'

'From walking or going to bed?'

'You followed me, didn't you...?' Lucy felt pretty stupid for not seeing the obvious and smelling a set up. 'You planned...' she moved her hands in an expressive fluttering motion and fixed him with a blue accusing glare '...this.'

'Such piercing insight,' he drawled, drawing a hissing sound of rage from between her clenched teeth. 'I did warn you what would happen if you came near my family.'

'So how is Gabby?'

'Back in school.' Gabby had assumed the day-early return was part of her punishment and Santiago had seen no reason to disabuse her of this notion. At least she was safely out of reach, though he doubted that his daughter would have found the scent of this woman's perfume quite so disturbing.

Sure, Santiago, you're so 'disturbed' that you can't think above the waist. Admit it like a man—you want her so bad you can taste it.

'Lucy's changed her mind—she's coming!' had been the words that had greeted him on his return that morning, making it pretty conclusive that his threats had backfired big time and Lucy Fitzgerald had lost no time calling his bluff—only he didn't bluff, as she would find out.

'I thought we could have a private little talk…' Not this little talk—Santiago was annoyed with himself for losing focus.

'We don't have anything to talk about and, for the record, I don't like being played. How did you know—' She stopped, feeling stupid. 'There wasn't an important call, was there?'

'Of course there was a call…and I imagine it will take a good thirty minutes.'

'Imagine or know!'

He met her angry glare with a lazy, insolent smile. 'What's the problem, Lucy—you can dish it out but can't take it?'

Her chin went up at the challenge. 'Dish it out?' she echoed, her blue gaze falling from his. 'I don't know what you mean,' she denied, thinking, *He knows…* The realisation that he had seen through their act was, she realised, almost a relief. She expelled a long sigh—no more pouting! With all the sexy stuff she hadn't felt like herself all evening— 'herself' being cool, blonde and in control.

This evening she'd been blonde and continually on the edge of losing any semblance of control. This man pressed all her buttons and made her feel the victim's rage she had thought she had conquered long ago.

She felt a twang of guilt, which turned into pity for Ramon—she could not imagine his brother seeing this as a bit of harmless fun.

'I am presuming that the overacting this evening was for my benefit?' An image of her stroking his brother's arm, a relatively innocent action if it had been anyone but this woman, drifted into his head and he snarled, 'Ever heard of subtlety?'

Lucy's head lifted and she read the contempt and anger etched in the sculpted lines of his hard-boned face.

'I presume this was to drive up the price.'

Her eyes widened—so he didn't know.

He saw her reaction and gave a thin smile. 'Another language you speak fluently...money.'

It occurred to Lucy as she sucked in a breath that she had played her part a bit too well—he was looking at her with a level of loathing that she struggled to be objective about.

'And did it work?' she wondered, hiding the stab of irrational hurt that threatened to make her well up behind her amused smile. The opinion of a self-righteous jerk, she reminded herself, was no reason to feel bad. In fact the time to worry was when a man like him started approving of you.

'No, there is no extra money on the table—there is no money.'

She pursed her lips into a pout and took what she hoped came across as a fearless step towards him. Thrusting one hip out, she planted her hands on her thighs and fixed him with a smile that deepened as she heard the distinct sound of his teeth grinding.

'Pity...still, sometimes the satisfaction of a job well done is reward in itself.'

'I have no idea if some bad experience turned you poisonous or if you were just born that way because, to be frank, the nature-nurture argument does not interest me.'

Inside seething, Lucy adopted an air of amused interest, watching the muscles along his strong jawline ripple.

'And I can take anything you can throw at me.' Brave

words, or should that be reckless? Lucy just hoped they would not come back to bite her.

'We'll see, shall we...?'

Sheer stubbornness made her retain eye contact. It saved running the risk of not being able to look away. His black stare had a disturbingly hypnotic quality.

Her pounding heart drowned out the lonely cry of a hunting owl overhead. The atmosphere was suddenly thicker than the thick emerald-green moss that grew along the riverbank, the moss her heels had sunk into as she'd walked to the bridge... Lucy felt as though she were sinking now. She swallowed past the constriction in her throat and, doing her best to look amused, met his black stare. He probably got some sadistic kick from seeing people squirm. No, she thought, there was no 'probably' about it.

She was aware that anything she said now might be construed as a challenge...and he was obviously a man who could not resist any opportunity to prove himself superior. He was pathetic, she told herself, though actually *pathetic* was about the most inappropriate term imaginable to describe the man standing there. He oozed a raw masculinity. There was something raw and elemental about him that made her traitorous heart skip a beat and her mouth dry and her knees weak.

A lot of other things were going on that she didn't even want to think about right now. *Deep breaths, Lucy...deep breaths.*

He held her eyes with a steady stare and watched the colour in her face fluctuate. Her skin fascinated him, so creamy he wanted to feel it to see if it felt as soft and satiny as it looked. He wanted to feel her naked underneath him. He had wanted it from the moment he had set eyes on her and, damn her, she had known it.

His chest swelled. He had never wanted a woman this

much in his life, so badly that he could taste it. He wanted to taste her so badly that... He embraced his anger just to stay in control.

Lucy sucked in a deep, wrathful breath and blurted, 'You are one manipulative—'

He moved so fast that it seemed that one moment he was standing several feet away, the next he was beside her with his finger poised a whisper away from her parted lips. She felt the pressure building inside and felt totally helpless to do anything about it.

'Think very carefully before you continue, Lucy. I am not my brother and I am not in the habit of turning the other cheek.'

'You mean you haven't mastered meek—imagine my amazement,' she drawled, slapping his hand away and taking a shaky step back.

Her heart was beating so hard it felt it might explode from her chest; the simple act of drawing air into her lungs required conscious effort... The musky scent of his warm skin lingered tantalisingly in her quivering nostrils.

He laughed. The sound was not unattractive; actually nothing was unattractive about him but his personality.

'Whereas you have.'

She gritted her teeth in response to the silky sarcasm of his retort and wrapped her arms around herself.

His brow furrowed as he watched her shiver. 'You're cold.'

He faked solicitude well, but Lucy recognised this new tactic for what it was—an attempt to soften her up. She knew that she was not the sort of woman who brought out the protective instincts in the opposite sex. She was not small or delicate and she did not consider this a bad thing. She had never envied the fragile little creatures that made men feel macho and strong.

'Look on the bright side—I might get pneumonia and die. Problem solved.'

A spasm of impatience tightened the hard contours of his jaw. 'Do not be stupid.' But she wasn't, anything but; the evening had proved that he had underestimated Miss Lucy Fitzgerald.

For 'stupid' Lucy translated 'anyone who didn't act as though his every word was engraved in stone'. She watched as he began to shrug off his jacket. The shirt he wore underneath was white with a subtle silver stripe and in the moonlight it was possible to see the lean shape of his body beneath it as he held out the jacket towards her.

She lowered her gaze but not before her insides had dissolved.

'You've got to be joking.'

His face was in darkness now, but bands of moonlight fell across his body. 'You find old-fashioned courtesy amusing.' His hand smoothed the contrasting silk lining of the jacket he had shrugged off.

'In the light of the fact you've spent the entire evening being as rude as hell to me…yes, actually, I do!'

Lucy planted her hands on her hips, her breasts under the red silk heaving as she glared up at him. 'You know something—I feel sorry for you!'

'Is that a fact?' he drawled, sounding bored. 'I suppose it's too much to hope you are not going to tell me why I am an object of pity in your eyes?'

'Because people like you—'

'People like me?'

'Sorry, I forgot, there are no people like you—you're special,' she drawled, sketching speech marks in the air. Her mocking smile faded as she added in a voice that shook with contempt, 'But actually you're not. Living in a castle and having pots of money makes you lucky—not special.'

'And you were born on the wrong side of the tracks forced to live off your wits? I don't think so,' he drawled.

Lucy blinked, but recovered quickly. 'I don't live in a castle.'

'And the Fitzgeralds are paupers, I suppose?'

Her blue gaze grew frosty. 'Leave my family out of this,' she warned fiercely.

This display of protectiveness struck him as ironic. 'Like you did? Did it ever occur to you to consider how your actions would affect them? How do you think they feel when they see you use your body and beauty as a weapon?'

Lucy laughed, finding the accusation particularly ironic when she was standing here struggling to control her breathing. *If only!*

'What can I say? I'm a shallow and superficial person.'

'You're…' He lunged without warning and grabbed her by the waist, the other hand went to the nape of her neck, his fingers pushing into her hair as he pulled her into him.

Panic made her struggle but then his mouth was on hers and her resistance melted, *she* melted; the arm banded around her narrow waist took her weight as she went limp.

He sank his teeth into the plump fullness of her lower lip, sighing as she moaned. The heat of his body penetrated the silk of her dress…nothing she was feeling was like anything she had experienced before.

'I really want to taste you.'

His smoky voice shivered through her body, awakening an answering need deep inside her. Using what strength she had to force her heavy lips open, she looked up at him with passion-glazed blue eyes.

'Yes,' she breathed huskily. 'Please.'

He kissed her deeply, his warm lips seductive, his probing tongue shockingly intimate, but it was the contrast of soul-piercing tenderness and ravenous hunger of the carnal assault on her senses that drew a series of soft moans from Lucy's throat.

Overwhelmed by the need his touch awoke, she wound her arms vine-like around his neck and kissed him back hard, meeting his tongue with her own.

The shocking rock-hard imprint of his erection as it ground into her belly excited her incredibly, making her gasp and moan, giving herself over totally to the wild hunger in her blood as the passion generated between them burned hotter. His mouth demanded more and she struggled to give it.

His hands moved down her body, moulding her against him, as Lucy's hands slid over his shoulders feeling the hard ridges of muscle through his clothes feeling the racing of her pulse, feeling his heartbeat, the two sounds becoming one.

The desperation of their soft moans and murmurs grew more frantic and uncontrolled until finally Santiago pulled back.

It took a few seconds for sanity to return. When it did the shocking realisation of what she had just done hit Lucy. She stood staring at him as she shook her head in denial, unable to accept the need he had awoken inside, the confusing tangle of emotions that the kiss had shaken loose.

He said nothing. The shadows across his face accented the strong planes and fascinating hollows. Just looking at him made her ache to touch him. 'You think that proves anything?' she challenged.

'It proved that we'd be pretty sensational in bed.'

She gave a scared little gasp and just ran.

When Ramon returned she was waiting in the car. He was terribly apologetic about the wait and didn't seem to notice anything unusual about her silence.

CHAPTER SIX

'RELAX,' Ramon recommended as Lucy looked nervously over her shoulder. 'You won't see him.'

That assurance was the only reason she was here—that and Ramon's promise of a ride on a pure-bred Arab, which she had been unable to resist.

Though she'd managed to do so until Ramon, correctly interpreting her reluctance, had promised his brother would not be there. 'So there's no need to be nervous.'

Her pride stung, she had retorted hotly, 'Your brother does not make me nervous. I simply find him...' At a loss to explain even to herself the way the man made her feel, she finished lamely, 'He won't be there.'

'No chance,' Ramon had promised, coaxing, 'Come on, the least I can do is give you the ride I promised. You've fulfilled your side of the bargain and, yes, don't worry,' he soothed, predicting her interruption, 'I know you don't want to carry on with our plan... You are sure about that?'

'Quite sure.'

'Pity, I was having fun. Oh, well.' Ramon gave a philosophical shrug. 'It's not all bad—you really got to Santiago.'

Not nearly as much as he got to me.

'Did I?' she said, getting hot as she thought of his hard, lean, ardent body pressing her...his warm breath... She sucked in a steadying breath and thought, *Keep it together, Lucy. The man kissed you—big deal!*

'Well, he was as rude as hell to you.'

'I assumed that was normal for him.'

Ramon shook his head. 'Big brother is always polite even when he's mad as hell. He has this way of letting you know you've messed up without raising his voice.'

'I feel so special.'

'You still sure you don't want to carry it on?'

'I don't. Sorry, Ramon, but I'm here to help Harriet and that doesn't leave much time to make myself a sitting target for your delightful brother's insults.'

Actually she did have time, as Harriet had pointed out when she had heard Lucy knock back Ramon's offer to go out.

'I appreciate what you're doing, Lucy, but even convicted prisoners are allowed time off for good behaviour and, besides, you're giving me an inferiority complex. The place has never looked so immaculate.'

Lucy had allowed herself to be persuaded...perhaps a little too easily?

'Ah, well...but it's all good. You made such an impression that no matter who I date is going to seem an improvement, so it's win-win for me.'

Lucy's lips quivered. 'I'm so glad to have been of help.' The sarcasm passed over Ramon's head. 'You are sure your brother won't be around?' She wasn't scared of bumping into him, it was simply a matter of common sense. She hated spiders so she wasn't going to wander into a room where she might encounter one.

'I told you Santiago rides before anyone is up. He's already done half a day's work before breakfast. The man's a machine, not human—he might not even sleep at all.'

Lucy did not share the admiration in Ramon's voice. 'Or maybe he can't sleep because he has a guilty conscience?'

The spiky comment drew a laugh from Ramon. 'Most people think Santiago is one of the good guys.'

Lucy snorted.

'That's Santiago's horse, Santana,' Ramon said as she walked to the stall containing the massive magnificent black stallion she remembered from her first meeting with Santiago… Was that really only four days ago?

It seemed like a lifetime ago.

The animal rolled his eyes, showing the whites as Ramon caught the hand she had extended to the animal and pulled her back. 'Not a good idea. He's a bit unpredictable.' *Like his master*, Lucy thought, remembering that kiss again and shivering. Jaw clenched with the effort, she pushed the memory away.

A few sleepless nights ago she had finally decided to cut herself some slack, realising that the only reason she had kissed him back like some sort of sex-starved bimbo was because she was—the sex-starved bit anyhow. She had been living the life of a nun and that was not normal or healthy.

When you thought about it, their kiss had been inevitable. It had certainly not been some life-changing experience, just the result of bad timing and hormones.

It had made her realise that what she needed was some balance in her life, and while she was not about to sign on with a dating agency or start attending speed-dating evenings— both suggestions from helpful family members—she was not going to actively avoid the possibility of a relationship. Rather, as her mum poetically phrased it, she was going to put herself out there.

If Friday night had proved anything it had proved she did after all have a libido. Her full lips twisted into a bitter smile—it was just a pity that she didn't have good taste!

She shook her head and tuned back in time to hear Ramon say, '…and not very fond of anyone but his master. Now how about Sapphire?' He drew Lucy towards a chestnut pure-bred Arab filly several stalls away from the black stallion. 'She's a lovely girl with very good manners.' Ramon held out his hand to offer a treat to the horse.

'She's lovely,' Lucy agreed, patting the animal. She placed a hand to her stomach as another of the cramps that had started an hour or so earlier made her catch her breath. The pain passed and she forgot about it as her attention strayed to the animal in the stall. 'Have you ever ridden Santana?'

Ramon laughed and shook his head. 'Santiago would have my skin if I tried. He doesn't share. You really have a way with horses.'

'My father bred racehorses as a hobby—we all ride. He put me on the back of my first horse when I was two and led me on a thoroughbred when I was six.' She broke off as Ramon lifted a hand to his head. 'Are you all right?'

Ramon shook his head. 'Fine, fine…I just need…' He flashed her a tight half smile and said, 'I'll be back in a minute. Tomas here will look after you.'

The groom Ramon hailed smiled and saddled up both horses, and when he realised that she knew what she was doing, left her alone.

'Abandoned,' she said, burying her face in the filly's neck.

She patted the gentle filly, who was tethered beside Ramon's mount—a good-looking Arab—and, pushing up the sleeve of her shirt, glanced at her watch.

'Great!' She gave a hissing sound of frustration and stomped up the aisle between the stalls. What was Ramon doing?

At this rate she would miss out on her ride altogether. She had left Harriet some sandwiches for lunch, but if her bored friend was left alone too long she knew that she wouldn't be able to resist starting the round of chores without her and probably put back her recovery several weeks in the process.

She was half tempted to take the pretty filly out alone and— The sound of hooves connecting with the wooden panel of a door interrupted her chain of thought.

'Hello, boy,' she said, walking to the stall where the stallion was pacing restlessly up and down. The animal pawed the ground and rolled his eyes. Lucy smiled and held out a hand fearlessly towards him, murmuring softly.

With a whinny the animal came forward, bending his head towards her as he pawed the floor.

'My, you're a handsome boy,' she soothed, finding it easy to identify with the animal's restless impatience. 'You need a run, don't you? So do I,' she added with a sigh. 'Have you been neglected? I wish I could…' She stopped, a slow smile spreading over her face as she thought, *Why not?*

Despite any number of answers surfacing in response to her silent question, the reckless idea took hold until by the time she had saddled the animal she had rationalised her decision to the point where she was actually doing the horse's true owner a favour—a beautiful creature like this needed exercise.

She did not doubt her ability to handle him: she had grown up around horses, she was a better than good rider and she had a natural affinity for all animals.

Her confidence seemed justified as she walked the animal around the exercise yard a couple of times before taking the path that Ramon had said led to a great gallop over open ground.

'We are a school, not a prison. We do not chain our girls to their beds and I can assure you our security is more than adequate. However, if a girl wants to run away…well, it is hard to prevent her.'

Santiago was not impressed by the logic and even less by what the school deemed an appropriate punishment for the crime. He clenched his jaw and struggled to moderate his response, aware his own school days had coloured his views of the educational world.

At seven he had been sent away to a school where bullying was endemic and the teachers had turned a blind eye to the activities of a group of sadistic pupils.

'Is not excluding someone who has tried to run away rather playing into her hands?' It certainly seemed to Santiago that the only lesson his daughter had learnt was run away and they sent you home as a punishment, which was exactly where she'd been heading when they'd caught up with her at the bus station.

A bus station where she had rubbed shoulders with... His hand bunched into fists as he brought this line of thought to a screaming halt.

His blood ran cold when he thought of his eleven-year-old daughter wandering around alone in a city. Gabby might think of herself as very grown up, and in some ways she was, but in others his daughter was very young for her age, something he was glad of, but it made her vulnerable.

'Gabby's behaviour has been unacceptable—'

'I find it unacceptable that you apparently have no idea why my daughter felt the need to run away.'

'Teenage girls—'

'My daughter is eleven.'

'Of course and as you know I was not comfortable with her skipping a year...a bright girl, of course...but...' Combating his growing irritation, Santiago tuned out the rest of a speech that when condensed read 'not my fault'. His tone cold and clipped, he finally interrupted.

'So Miss Murano will accompany her on the train.'

'Yes, and you will arrange for her to be picked up at your end?'

Santiago, who intended to pick his errant daughter up himself, grunted an affirmative and put the phone down.

He was leaving his study when he almost collided with his head groom. The man was so incoherent that it took him several minutes to make sense of what he was saying. When he did he experienced a flash of blind fury.

'So the English lady took out Santana and she headed which way?'

Santiago hit the ground running, no longer keeping his anger in check but releasing it to keep the nightmare images floating in his head at bay... This was not happening again.

It could not!

His brother's horse was fortuitously saddled and waiting in the yard. Santiago loosed the rein from the post it was looped over and, vaulting into the saddle, dug in his heels. The animal responded to the urgency and leapt responsively forward.

As they galloped onto the trail Santiago planned the words that would annihilate her. He was visualising the humility he would see in her attitude before he eventually wrung her lovely neck when his own horse, his mouth flecked with white, his black mane flying, galloped past.

An icy fist clenched in his chest and the images of retribution evaporated. He soothed his own spooked mount, sternly checking the animal's desire to follow the stallion, and rode on. The scene that met his eyes when he emerged from the forested strip was his worst nightmare.

He dismounted, leaving the animal to graze as he ran to where the still figure lay, dread clutching in his belly.

CHAPTER SEVEN

IT WAS happening again.

Not déjà vu, more a waking nightmare.

His face was like carved granite as he made himself look at her. Her face was pale; she looked like an effigy carved from ice.

She would be growing cold and there would be blood. He remembered the blood in his dreams; he saw it often. Saw the scarlet flecks on her mouth and knew it was his fault because Magdalena, sweet, gentle Magdalena had been trying to impress him.

Lucy heard the crunch of footsteps on the hard ground getting closer as she lay there, her chest burning as she tried to replace the air the fall had knocked out of her lungs. It hurt, but it was nothing more than she deserved, she decided, furious with herself for making such an amateurish mistake. Anyone could fall, but to let go of the reins when you came off…now that was stupid!

She waited for another of the painful stomach cramps to pass—this one was even more painful than the one that had hit her when the horse had stumbled—before she prised her eyelids apart and saw the shiny Italian leather shoes. She didn't need to go any further up the leg of grey tailored trousers… She knew who was standing there.

Of all the people who could have discovered her in this ignominious position, it had to be him.

The surge of intense relief Santiago had felt when he saw her blue-veined eyelids flutter against her pale waxen cheek was submerged by the equally strong blast of white-hot fury that rapidly succeeded it. When she began to move his entire body shook with the effort of keeping his feelings in check, feelings that had been shaken loose by the sight of her seemingly lifeless body.

'Keep still!' he yelled, fighting his way through the memories that crowded in on him and forcing himself to think here and now...think potential spinal injuries?

Ignoring the terse instruction—did the man have to make everything sound like an order?—Lucy, determined not to lie there like a stranded fish while he looked down at her with disdain from an Olympian height, pulled herself up into a sitting position.

She clamped her teeth over the groan as the effort of the simple action caused a fine layer of cold perspiration to break out over the surface of her skin.

The immediate problem was breathing.

'Just winded...' she rasped between gasps, her voice barely audible as she struggled with the fastener of the helmet, then, exhausted by the effort, she lay it in her lap.

Santiago's dark eyes moved from her pale trembling fingers to the cloud of silver-white hair that, released from the confines of the helmet, spilled down her back unbidden. The memory of feeling those glossy strands sliding through his fingers like silk surfaced... He pushed but the tactile memory lingered so inexplicably strong that his fingertips tingled.

Lucy plucked a piece of grass from her once pristine white shirt, very conscious of the angry figure who towered over her. Why didn't he say something...? Finally unable to stand the simmering silence any longer, she croaked, 'I've got grass stains on my shirt.'

With a snarl of disbelief, Santiago dropped down into a crouch beside her.

'Grass stains!' he ejaculated, taking the helmet from her trembling fingers and resisting the growing compulsion to press one of her slim white hands between his palms. This woman did not need comforting, she needed therapy.

Needed kissing.

'*Por Dios!* If you can't say anything sensible, shut up!'

Lucy, who could not have said anything even had she wanted to, swallowed past the aching emotional occlusion in her throat and clamped her teeth down on her trembling lower lip.

'This thing...' His voice faded as he laid the helmet to one side with exaggerated care. He inhaled and levelled a burning glare at the top of her blonde head as he fought for control. 'This thing probably saved your life. You were lucky.' It was not always the way... His heavy eyelids lowered partially, concealing the bleakness in the dark depths as the brutal inescapable images played in his head.

For a moment the silence hung between them, broken when Lucy gave a strangled sob she turned into a cough before pressing her face into her cupped palms. 'Don't dramatise,' she mumbled, unconsciously repeating the phrase her father had always said when she became overemotional as a child.

That brought his head up with a jerk. 'Dramatise!' He swore in his native tongue and sucked in a wrathful breath as he dragged a hand over his ebony hair. 'You want to see dramatic...?'

She lifted her face, her slightly dazed electric-blue eyes connecting with his, and Santiago lost track of his train of thought. Despite the tough-guy act she looked as he felt, and the petulant rebuttal seemed to have exhausted her. All the fight was gone, leaving her looking defenceless and vulnerable and several million miles away from the seductress his brother needed saving from.

With her defences stripped away her luminous beauty shone through: perfect bone structure, flawless skin... It was hard to look at such perfection and remain unmoved. As he stared he felt his anger drain away, leaving him feeling as if his armour had been stripped away... He felt suddenly exposed... He pushed away the thought. The only thing that was exposed was her inability to think beyond her own instant gratification.

Lucy sat there, her breath coming in painful uneven rasps, chin on her chest, her eyes lifted to the man squatting casually on the balls of his feet beside her. As always, he gave off the impression of elegant good taste overlaid by an aura of raw sexual magnetism that always made the details of what he was wearing secondary. Today it was an outfit more appropriate to the office than riding—a pale grey suit, crisp white shirt and silk tie, all classic and tasteful.

As their eyes connected the anger that was rolling off him hit like a physical force.

'You shouldn't be moving,' Santiago snarled, thinking in the same breath he had to stop her before she caused permanent damage and it would serve her right if she did.

Practically speaking, if she chose to ignore him, short of flattening her with a rugby tackle and pinning her to the ground—an image that his imagination tended to linger unhealthily over—Santiago recognised that all he could do was watch.

'Just because I'm saying something doesn't mean it's the wrong thing to do, Lucy.'

Lucy blinked, horrified to feel the sting of hot tears behind her eyes. She was proof against his insults but the unexpected gruff gentleness she heard in his voice sliced through her defences like a hot knife through ice cream.

She bit her quivering lip, held up a hand in mute appeal and husked a breathless plea. She couldn't cry—her tears would be something else for him to curl his lip contemptuously at. 'I just need a minute…to get my breath back.'

Santiago opened his mouth to speak, then closed it again and tilted his head sharply in acquiescence before rising to his feet in one fluid motion. He walked away feeling an urgent need to put some distance between them.

Running one hand over his jaw, he reached for his phone with the other. The woman, he decided, punching in a number with unwanted viciousness, was amazing. Considering the circumstances, he had been bloody restrained and yet with one look from her swimming blue eyes she managed to simultaneously look like some innocent virgin and make him feel like a bullying tyrant—it was quite a skill.

In the periphery of her vision Lucy was conscious of him pacing a few feet away while speaking tersely into a mobile phone. When he dropped down beside her once more a few moments later her breathing was normal and more importantly she was no longer on the brink of a teary outburst.

'Better?'

She nodded in response to his abrupt enquiry and said in her head, *Suck it up Lucy, keep it together.*

Santiago remained sceptical. The alarming rattle had gone, but her breath still seemed to be coming rather fast; she was almost hyperventilating.

Aware that it might appear he was staring at the heaving contours of her full breasts, which he was, but with total clinical objectivity—not everyone might get the objectivity—Santiago dragged his gaze clear.

'Your leg.' For the first time he saw the damage done to the well-worn jodhpurs that clung to her hips and the long lines of her magnificent legs. Along the outside of the right leg the fabric was torn, from thigh to ankle it gaped, revealing a section of bare skin.

His fingertips barely brushed her calf before she snatched her leg up. 'It's fine—a graze.' With a dismissive shrug she tucked the limb underneath her and concentrated on the pain in her calf to stop herself thinking about how much she had wanted him to touch her.

Perhaps she had had a knock on the head?

Friday night it had been the glass of wine, or so she had told herself through the long, sleepless, guilt-racked night that had followed, and now it was a bang on the head—what excuse would she have the next time she found herself craving this man's touch?

There isn't going to be a next time.

He arched a sardonic brow and shrugged. 'If you say so.' The doctor might have other thoughts. The groove above his nose deepened as he glanced down the track—where was the doctor?

'I do,' she said firmly.

As he replayed the phone conversation of moments before in his head the oddness of Ramon's response to his request to call for a doctor struck Santiago for the first time.

'Good idea,' his half-brother had said without asking why or for whom medical assistance was required.

Hand on the back of her neck, she angled a cautious look at Santiago's face. She knew the lull in hostilities would not last; this reprieve was definitely only temporary. Even when she hadn't ridden off on his favourite horse he couldn't open his mouth without being snide and cutting.

Now she actually was in the wrong the comfort of the moral high ground was a dim and distant memory... *Oh, God.* She took a deep breath and thought, *Take it like a man, Lucy. Bite the bullet and when you run out of clichés, apologise.* She closed her eyes and thought, *What the hell was I thinking?*

She hated admitting she was wrong at the best of times, but admitting it to Santiago made it a hundred times worse. She could take his anger—it was the knowing she deserved it that she struggled with.

Crazily, with all the legitimate things she had to stress about, it was the irrational one that was giving Lucy the most problems. She knew he couldn't read her mind—he just liked to leave the impression he was all-seeing, all-knowing—yet she couldn't shake the conviction that he was going to look at her and know she had spent the last few nights fantasising about him.

'Did Santana run home?' she asked in a small voice.

Santiago's head jerked towards her, his silent anger more articulate than a stream of abuse.

Unable to take her eyes off the errant muscle that was clenching and unclenching spasmodically in his cheek, in the face of his fury she leapt to the obvious conclusion. She began to shake her head in denial.

'Oh, no, he isn't injured…!' The thought of being responsible for an injury to that beautiful and expensive animal… God, no wonder he looked as if he wanted to throttle her. 'He's…' Her blue eyes widened in her milk-pale face as she whispered fearfully, 'He's not dead, is he?'

'Would you care if he was?'

A sound close to a whimper emerged from her throat and Santiago, who never had been comfortable with kicking someone when they were down, took pity on her obvious distress.

'I have no idea how Santana is,' he admitted, before adding with a scowl, 'But he was so spooked when I saw him that it will probably take a week for him to calm down and an army to catch him.' He lied, well aware that the animal would have gone straight back to his stable.

'I'm so, so sorry.'

'For stealing a valuable horse, for proving you can't handle anything bigger than a donkey or for getting caught?'

Her blue eyes flew wide. 'I didn't steal anything!'

He arched a brow at the protest. 'Tell that to the police.'

She regarded him in horror. 'You wouldn't call the police.'

He smiled and arched a sardonic brow. 'You think?'

Was he serious? Lucy refused to let him see that his threat had scared her. 'I think you're a total bastard.'

'Not illegal last time I researched the subject.' He gave a nasty smile. 'Unlike horse stealing.'

'I wasn't stealing your horse, I was just…riding him.'

'Why?'

She blinked, struggling after the fact to explain even to herself the impulse that had made her take the horse out. 'Why not?' She shrugged.

'So this is a case of anything Lucy sees and wants Lucy has to have even if it belongs to someone else?' Didn't she understand that a person could not have anything they wanted? There were rules, like the unwritten one that said a man did not muscle in on his brother's girlfriend—did it count when you'd be saving your brother from a terrible fate? Did the unwritten rule stand when the brother in question didn't possess your own ability to keep your sexual appetites and your emotions separate from a terrible fate?

Lucy saw where he was going with this. 'Ramon doesn't belong to anyone else, even though you went out of your way to make it seem like he does.'

Santiago's scowl deepened. He had thrown Carmella, with her crush on Ramon, into the mix hoping she would offer a distraction with her youth and innocence. He was ready to admit that his plan had failed miserably and he felt guilty for using the kid.

'But Denis Mulville did.' What chance would any wife have if Lucy Fitzgerald decided she wanted a man?

At the name Lucy's face lost any colour it had regained. The condemnation on his face was nothing new. She had seen similar expressions on the faces of virtually everyone she met four years ago, and some of those faces had belonged to people she had considered friends.

At the centre of a storm of ill will Lucy had felt every cruel word and jeer until she had taught herself not to care about the opinion of others. People could and would think what they liked, but so long as she knew the truth that was all that mattered…at least in theory.

Reality meant that there had still been nights when she had cried herself to sleep and days when she had longed to put her side of the story, but she had maintained her dignified silence even after the gagging order was lifted.

Not once had she yelled at one of her accusers—'I never slept with the man. He was a creep!'

As she did now, ironically to someone whose good opinion meant nothing to her, someone who dismissed her words with a contemptuous shrug.

There was a chance, Santiago thought, that she told the literal truth—a man who got her in bed would not be likely to fall asleep!

'How did you justify breaking up a family?' A hissing sound of disgust issued from between his clenched teeth as he dragged a hand through his ebony hair. 'Do you tell yourself that he wouldn't look at you if he had a happy marriage? That there wouldn't have been an affair if the marriage hadn't been in trouble to begin with—isn't that what the other woman always says?'

'You tell me! You seem the expert on the subject.'

She broke off, wincing as she experienced a stomach cramp a lot sharper than any of the previous ones. She closed her eyes and gritted her teeth. If she threw up in front of this man the humiliation factor would be off the scale.

Lucy lifted her head, breathing through the pain.

'What's wrong?'

'Nothing!' she snapped.

The beads of perspiration that had broken out over the pale skin of her brow suggested otherwise.

'I know I shouldn't have taken the horse, but I was waiting for Ramon and Santana obviously needed exercise and you hadn't bothered to exercise him...'

'So this is my fault?'

The note of fake comprehension caused the spots of dark colour on her pale cheeks to deepen. 'No, but—'

'But you,' he cut back in a hard voice, 'saw an opportunity of scoring points because I warned you off—'

'No!'

'Then I can only assume you wanted my attention. You didn't have to steal my valuable horse in order to get that—if you wanted to be kissed all you had to do was ask.'

She looked at him with simmering dislike. 'Not in this life!' she pronounced with an emphatic shake of her head. She swallowed and pressed a hand to her mouth.

'What's wrong?'

'I'm feeling a bit nauseous,' she admitted, thinking about Ramon's abrupt departure and wondering if the two could be connected... They had shared that smoked salmon sandwich...?

'Let me look in your eyes,' he said, taking her chin in his fingers.

'I don't have a head injury.'

His fingers fell away. 'Do you remember what happened?'

'Of course I remember what happened—I came off.'

'Got thrown.'

'All right, got thrown,' she gritted, thinking, *Go on, rub it in why don't you?* 'That's why I lost control when he got spooked by that little pig.' Actually it had been quite a large pig.

To hear one of the dangerous wild boar that lived in the woods dismissed with a disgusted grimace made him blink.

'I'm a good rider. I've been riding all my life.'

'And have you been falling off all your life?'

Struggling to combat the rising nausea, Lucy wiped the rash of damp off her forehead, managing to lift her head and fix him with a glare. 'I suppose you have never fallen off.' She pressed her hand to her mouth and thought, *Please do not let me throw up in front of him.*

The annoyance died from Santiago's face as he studied her pale features. 'You look terrible.'

And she felt terrible.

'Do you feel faint?'

At that moment she would have accepted a graceful, aesthetically pleasing swoon, but it wasn't an option. 'No, I don't feel faint, I feel...' She clapped a hand to her mouth, jumped to her feet and sprinted across the clearing. A few yards away she fell to her knees.

'You all right?'

She shrugged off the hand on her shoulder and got to her feet, unable to meet his eyes. 'Obviously I'm not all right.' The nausea was much easier to cope with than the humiliation of the situation... God, she wanted to die; he had actually held her hair away from her face!

Santiago was the very last person in the world she would have expected a display of such thoughtfulness from, or, for that matter, expected to possess such a strong stomach.

'Did you hit your head...lose consciousness?' Her creamy complexion was tinged with a greenish hue and she was visibly swaying like a young sapling in a breeze... Sheer bloody-minded stubbornness, he suspected, was the only thing keeping her upright.

'No, I...I was already...' Losing track of her rebuttal, her voice faded to a whisper as her eyes half closed.

Convinced now he was dealing with a concussion at the very least, Santiago was moving in to catch her when she opened her eyes, directing her wide-eyed cerulean stare directly at his face.

'It wasn't the fall. I've been feeling...off most of the morning.' Her brow furrowed; it was hard in retrospect to recall when it had started. Post smoked salmon, definitely.

The confession sparked his dormant anger into life. 'Of all the selfish...stupid...!' he blasted. 'So let me get this right—not only did you steal a horse you could not handle simply to thumb your nose at me, you did so while unwell.'

Lucy, who had been on the point of offering a shamed apology, lost all urge to admit she'd been wrong.

'I didn't know I was going to be sick...' Wincing at the unattractive whiney note in her voice, Lucy reached for the scarf she had wound around her neck that morning, intending to tie back her hair with it, and found it was gone...

'What is it now?' He watched cautiously as she bit her quivering lip and hoped she was not about to start throwing up again, though he conceded it was preferable to tears.

It was bizarre. He had always considered himself an even-tempered man, certainly not someone prone to mood swings, but with this woman he could feel a strong compulsion to throttle her and two seconds later an equally strong compulsion to offer her a shoulder to cry on.

'I lost my scarf...' She stopped as he looked at her as though she had gone mad and added, 'And I wasn't trying to thumb my...' Her forceful declaration came to an abrupt halt, she swallowed and thought, *My God, wasn't that exactly what I was doing?*

Something about this man made her want to score points: his aggressive sexuality, his self-righteous attitude, his smug conviction he was always right—no, actually, it was everything!

'I shouldn't have taken the horse…the biggest horse,' she tacked on before she could stop herself.

And once she'd begun it was impossible to stem the flow of words that spilled from her.

'The one that nobody else can handle, fastest, shiniest car…biggest bank balance…oh, and let's not forget the Olympian-class smug superiority. Do you ever stop competing? It's nothing short of a miracle that Ramon isn't riddled with insecurities.' She ran out of steam, dismay gradually seeping into her expression as she realised what she'd just said.

'Shiniest car?'

Her eyes fell.

'Is that how you see me—a boy with his toys…?'

She saw him with no clothes on, or she had in her erotic, shameful dreams. She closed her eyes and groaned. 'Oh, just call the police. I'll go quietly.' Sitting in a police cell had to be preferable to enduring his company.

'Don't worry, I am not going to call the police.'

She choked on her relieved sigh when he tacked on, 'I'll sack the groom. It was his responsibility and rules are rules.'

Her horrified blue eyes flew to his face. 'You wouldn't…' She stopped as she encountered an ironic look.

'And with my word being law and my reputation as a despot being at stake I need to make an example of someone,' he delivered straight-faced.

'Very funny. Oh, God, I'm going to be ill again.'

CHAPTER EIGHT

'There's no point waiting.'

The decision made, Santiago slid an assessing glance towards the woman who was now sitting with her back propped against a tree trunk looking very much like a wilting exotic flower. The last bout of vomiting had left her very weak.

Admiration was something he had never imagined he would feel about Lucy, but, you had to hand it to her, she did not complain.

She might be putting on a brave front but, guts or not, there was no way in the world she could make it under her own steam…but with his support she could sit in the saddle in front of him and they could be back at the *castillo* in a matter of minutes. They would be now if he hadn't assumed that help was on its way.

Santiago turned, clicking his fingers as he did so to bring the horse to him…only there wasn't a horse to bring. Ramon's gelding was nowhere in sight.

The expression on his face when he realised that the horse had wandered away would have made her laugh on any other occasion.

He swore softly under his breath.

'We've both lost a horse.'

His withering gaze swung her way. 'Thank you for pointing that out. It is most helpful.'

Head tilted to one side, he fixed her with a narrow-eyed assessing glance until Lucy, feeling increasingly self-conscious by his unblinking regard, snapped crankily. 'What? What's wrong?'

'I was just considering the options…'

Presuming he was about to share the details, she was taken totally by surprise by the abruptness of the action that followed his terse explanation. Lucy was so shocked that she offered no resistance when he almost casually lifted her into his arms—just a scream.

A moment later she managed a breathless, indignant, 'What are you doing?' Other than displaying strength that Lucy—who was not by anyone's standards a small woman— struggled hard not to find impressive. However, she had never had a single fantasy about being rescued and swept into the strong arms of a man—any man.

Especially not *this* man!

'Not wasting further time hanging around.' For assistance that seemed to be taking a long time coming.

Or asking permission before treating her like a sack of coal, she mused, giving a second shrill yelp as he moved, striding across the open ground towards the forest trail.

Lucy stared at his ear and held herself stiff, noticing the way his hair curled around it into the nape of his neck… strong neck. It was mid-morning but she could see the beginning of stubble on his jaw and cheek. It would feel… She paused mid-thought and gasped.

'I don't want to know!'

'Know what?'

Lucy's eyes fell away guiltily. 'Know how long it will be before you drop me.' Pleased with her quick recovery, she lifted her gaze just as he loosened his grip for a split second but enough to make her react instinctively out of self-preservation.

She grabbed him, one hand sliding under his unfastened jacket, the other around his neck.

'Breathing would be nice.'

There was an embarrassing delay before her brain, busy processing details like the warmth and lithe hardness of the warm male body she was crushed up against, reacted to his dry comment.

'Very funny,' she drawled, loosening her grip but not all the way—he was almost jogging now and the next time it might not be a joke. 'Will you put me down? This is ridiculous.' Almost as ridiculous as her reaction to a bit of muscle.

'Look, I'd love to argue the toss with you, but frankly I need all my breath. You're a lot heavier than you look.' Her weight was not the problem, but the soft yielding nature of the warm body that seemed to fit naturally into his was. Lucy Fitzgerald was not a woman who had sharp angles; she was not a woman that a man could be close to and not think about naked.

It was an image that Santiago, whose normal iron control when it came to such matters was at that moment absent, struggled to erase. In fact, he was struggling to think beyond the surge of hormones that made him want to lay her down on the warm mossy ground and... The sound of his harsh inhalation was drowned out by Lucy's indignant gasp.

'Are you calling me fat?'

The growl of desire growing low in his throat turned into an amused snort as, appreciating the irony, he quirked his lips into a twisted smile. He had called her many things that were worse, but it was the suggestion that she was overweight that rattled her.

'I may not be a skinny—'

A stone too heavy, according to the man from Hollywood who, at the height of her notoriety, had dangled the female lead in a new film with the proviso she lose that stone. It had

clearly not even crossed his mind, or for that matter her ju-
bilant agent's, that Lucy would say thanks but no thanks to
the chance of being the love interest to one of the industry's
most bankable stars.

'Sorry, but I can't act,' she had said to soften her refusal.

This, it had turned out, was not an obstacle and her ability
to look good in very little apparently more than compensated
for this minor deficiency. The scandal attached to her name
had apparently been deemed box-office gold.

'But I'm not about to starve myself so men like you can
feel macho hauling me around.'

'Dios mio!' He stopped dead and angled an astonished
stare at her indignant face.

As their eyes connected the amused exasperation in his
expression vanished, as did any temptation to defend himself against the accusation.

In his arms Lucy could feel his chest lifting as though
standing there were putting more stress on his heart than jogging along had; her own heart was fluttering like a trapped
bird in her chest cavity.

She told herself it was her weakened state that made her
tremble, unable to admit even to herself it was being the
focus of his febrile gaze that had sent her nervous system into
shocked overload. As for the impression that the air around
them was literally shimmering with a heat haze—that was
obviously a result of dehydration or fever.

'You have a perfect body and we both know it.'

Turning his attention abruptly back to the trail ahead, he
picked up pace—not a cold shower but the next best thing—
and wondered about the shock in her face. Such a reaction
seemed bizarre considering she was a woman who traded
on her looks and sensuality.

Silenced by the abrupt assessment, Lucy was almost glad
when the nausea and stomach cramps took her mind off the

molten stream of desire that had turned her into a breathless bundle of craving and reduced her brain function to zero.

When a short while later, or it might have been a long time, Lucy had lost track, he asked, 'Are you sulking?' Lucy thought it wise to warn him.

'No, I don't feel very well...' Her eyes were closed as she spoke but she could feel his dark gaze on her face.

Presumably she looked terrible because he started jogging faster. There was no way, she thought dully, that he could keep up this pace for much longer even if he was incredibly fit.

'Nearly there,' he murmured close to her ear. 'Hold on.'

'God, don't be nice to me,' she begged, wondering what alternative universe she had slipped into where Santiago made her feel safe and cared for. 'Or I'll cry.'

Tears would have left him unmoved but the plea touched him. He could not think of another woman he knew who would prefer to be yelled at than give in to tears. 'Shut up or I'll drop you.'

Lucy sketched a weak smile and forgot to hate him. 'Thank you. I suppose I am being very ungrateful.'

'Yes.'

'I'll try not to throw up on you...it's a beautiful suit,' she heard herself say, and wondered if, despite the fact she felt freezing cold, she had a fever. 'God, I'm never sick!' she groaned, vowing to show more sympathy in future to people who were physically more fragile than she was.

She was now and the sight of her poor pale face made him complete the last leg of the journey in record time.

By the time they reached the stableyard there was no question of it being illicit lust that made Lucy cling to him; she wasn't even aware that she was groaning softly into his shoulder.

He looked around the deserted yard, which normally at

this time of the day was a hive of activity, and felt his frustration grow.

He cut between the buildings built around a quadrangle and across the lawn, ignoring the burning of his shoulder muscles, spurred on by the soft moans of the woman he carried.

He walked straight through the massive double doors of the front entrance and into the vaulted hallway. It was empty. He opened his mouth to yell when Josef appeared. Normally insouciant Josef's eyes widened when he saw his boss with a semi-conscious woman in his arms.

'Where is my brother?'

'With the doctor. He's rather unwell.'

'Ramon is ill, too?' Santiago closed his eyes. Two invalids on his hands, one literally, and an errant daughter to collect from the station. When they spoke of it never raining but pouring, his was presumably the day they were referring to.

'Can I help with the young lady, sir?'

'No, you can get Martha and the new girl…Sabina, and ask them to come to the west-wing suite…inform the doctor he is required there and have the helicopter ready to take off in thirty minutes. Gabby is coming home early.'

Josef waited as he reeled off the instructions and then, with a nod, vanished. A man of few words, Josef; Santiago liked that about him.

'You're so pretty.'

Lucy blinked and pushed her way free of the last layers of sleep. The figure standing by the window came into focus. To her relief, it was not a hallucination—unless hallucinations spoke and wore braces.

She blinked at the small elfin features of Gabby.

'Thank you,' Lucy replied, easing herself carefully up on one elbow and turning her curious gaze around the room.

She had not been that interested in her surroundings the previous night when Santiago had brought her in here and relinquished her to the care of the doctor and the two women who had stayed with her during the night.

One of them had spoken perfect English, the other was the sweet girl who had cut her hand, both had been incredibly kind.

'I thought you were in school.'

'I ran away.'

Lucy was weak enough to feel a fleeting moment of sympathy for Santiago.

'What time is it?'

The furniture in the room that was massive enough to lose the enormous four-poster she was lying in was dark and heavy and looked like museum pieces. The stone walls were covered with tapestries and portraits of severe-looking historical persons. The personal touch of an arrangement of garden flowers in the gleaming copper bowl set in the empty cavernous fireplace filled the room with their scent and lightened the general museum-style gloom.

'It's two o'clock.'

Lucy was startled. She had fallen asleep in the early hours. 'Why didn't someone wake me?' She brushed her hair from her face and struggled to tear her eyes from the portrait of a hatchet-faced woman in a jewelled turban. The eyes looked spookily familiar, an ancestor presumably of the present incumbent. Clearly hauteur was not a new Silva characteristic, any more than the masterful nose.

'They said to let you and Sara sleep.'

Lucy yawned and dragged her attention back to the girl. 'Sara?' Her brow crinkled. Was she meant to know the name? At that moment she was struggling with her own.

'She's one of the maids. She ate some of the bad salmon that was for the cook's mother's cat, too.'

Struggling to follow this information overload, Lucy moistened her lips with her tongue—they felt dry and cracked—and recalled the smoked salmon and cream cheese bagel that Ramon had produced when she had said she couldn't possibly go riding until she had had her breakfast.

'I haven't eaten either but not to worry, I have it covered,' he had said, producing the breakfast treat wrapped in a linen napkin.

When she had laughed and conceded he had thought of everything she hadn't known that had included food poisoning! Could he have escaped unscathed?

'Ramon?'

'Oh, Uncle Ramon was much worse than you.'

'But he's better now?' Lucy was just relieved that Harriet, who she had cooked breakfast for before she went out to attend to the donkeys—six a.m. was not a time of the day that Lucy personally felt happy eating—had not shared the breakfast.

'I don't know. Ramon was really sick. He had to go to hospital.'

'Hospital!' Lucy exclaimed in alarm.

She nodded. '*Papá* said it serves him right for raiding the pantry.'

Gabby took a seat on the brocade bed cover using the crewel-work curtains that draped the bed for leverage.

Lucy discovered that she was wearing a long white Victorian-style nightgown in a fine, exquisitely embroidered fabric. Her memory of how she came to be wearing this period-looking piece was sketchy, but she was sure— almost—that Santiago had not been involved.

Having delivered her, he had immediately made himself scarce and she didn't blame him, though… Her brow furrowed. She did have a vague recollection of hearing a deep male voice and feeling cool fingers on her forehead at one point during the night, but that might have been part of a dream.

Running the flat of her hand down the gossamer-thin floaty sleeve of the nightdress, she lifted her gaze to find the child watching her. Santiago's daughter was a pretty little thing with a roundish face, big dark eyes and a cupid's bow mouth and dimpled cheeks—did she look like her dead mother?

'That's mine off Aunt Seraphina. Awful, isn't it? She always buys me stuff that's massive for me to grow into, but I never do.' The little sigh made Lucy smile—clearly the size thing was an issue with her.

'*Papá* says it's good to be petite but what does he know? He's a man and ten feet tall…' she grumbled, adding enviously, 'Like you. Is your hair real…not extensions?' She viewed the silken skein that framed Lucy's face with a mixture of curiosity and envy. 'I'd like to bleach my hair but *Papá* would kill me. It might be worth it, though,' she added with a grin. 'And who knows? It might be the final straw and they'll expel me this time.' She caught Lucy's quizzical look and added, 'I hate school.'

The description made Lucy think wistfully of the time when her own father had seemed the biggest thing in the world. She repressed a smile.

'The hair is all my own,' Lucy admitted, reaching for the water on the bedside table and taking a sip. Her throat felt dry and raw. 'Well, your *papá* is right—there's nothing wrong with being petite. I always wished I was.' But it was never good to be different and at this girl's age she had towered above her contemporaries.

'*Papá* is right…? Can I have that in writing?'

Lucy slopped water all down the front of the borrowed nightdress and turned to see Santiago standing framed in the doorway.

The sight of his tall dynamic figure sent a wild rush of energising adrenaline through her body. Dressed in a white tee shirt and jeans, his slicked wet hair suggesting he had just stepped out of the shower, he oozed a restless, edgy vitality.

He also looked sinfully gorgeous and Lucy didn't have the energy or for once the inclination to go through the entire 'sexy but not my type' routine... She was hopelessly attracted to him. Just sex, she told herself, drawing back from deeper examination of the tight knot of emotions lying like a leaden weight behind her breastbone.

'What are you doing here?' she quivered accusingly.

He arched a brow and said mildly, 'I live here.'

She flushed and heard the words *king of the castle* in her head as she followed the direction of his quizzical gaze. It led to the silk-covered pillow she was clutching to her chest like a shield.

Lucy had no recollection of grabbing it and equally she had no intention of letting it go, though as shields went it was about as effective as a feather in a storm against the illicit lust that hardened her nipples to thrusting prominence beneath thin, fine fabric.

'I didn't wake her, *Papá*, honest, did I?'

Santiago levered his tall lean frame off the wall, not ten feet but muscle packed, and very impressive.

'No, I was awake,' Lucy lied, and received a beam of gratitude in return.

'What is this—a conspiracy?' He appeared faintly amused as he turned to the child and added, 'Run along, kiddo, you are already in enough trouble and Miss Fitzgerald is tired.' He turned to Lucy and said, 'The doctor is with the maid who was sick, too. I just called by to let you know he'll be here when he's finished with her.'

Tired... Miss Fitzgerald, he thought, his hooded glance

skimming her paper-pale face, looked like some Hollywood version of a sexy vampire—fragile but deadly.

Once he started looking it was hard to stop. She was the most dramatically beautiful woman he had ever seen. A bare scrubbed face only emphasised the crystal purity of her perfectly symmetrical features; the skin, stretched tighter after her sleepless night, across the beautiful bones was satiny smooth; her sleepless pallor and the dark smudges made the colour of her eyes appear even more dramatic than usual.

It was a major improvement to the way she had looked the night before. Last night she had looked… Struggling to hold onto his train of thought, Santiago narrowed his eyes in concentration and broke contact with her sapphire stare.

The muscles along his angular jawline quivered as he recalled the attitude of the doctor, who turned out to be not the family friend but a locum who seemed barely shaving, standing in. The man, having already called an ambulance for Ramon, had seemed inclined to underplay the severity of Lucy's condition.

To Santiago it had seemed logical to err on the side of caution and he had been far from convinced by the doctor's assertion that staying where she was and reviewing the situation tomorrow was the best course of action in Lucy's case.

He had been proved right and Santiago had been ready to admit as much this morning. The doctor deserved an apology and he respected the fact the other man had not rolled over and said yes sir—a response that Santiago encountered all too often.

The doctor's response to his apology had been a good-natured shrug.

'I've been called worse and threatened with worse,' he'd said. 'Though not from anyone who looked quite so capable of carrying through with the threats,' he'd admitted with a rueful roll of his eyes. 'It's hard for people to be objective when they are emotionally involved.'

Santiago had been midway through assuring the man that he was not in any way emotionally involved with the patient, that in point of fact he barely knew the woman, when he had realised that, the more he protested, the more he sounded like someone in denial.

He had let the subject drop.

'She's been asleep for hours and hours.' Gabby relinquished her perch on the bed but only took one step towards the door before her curiosity got the better of her. 'And the doctor says that no one can catch anything. You're not…contagious…?' She glanced towards her father, who nodded. 'And all we need to do is maintain…' Again the glance.

'Basic good hygiene.'

'Basic good hygiene. Did you really ride Santana?'

Lucy's eyes flew guiltily to Santiago and she discovered with a little shocking thrill that he was staring at her. Guilty heat poured into her face. 'I…it was a…mistake.'

'And you fell off?'

Take it like a man, Lucy, she told herself. 'Yes, I fell off.' Some people might call it bad luck and some, she thought, flashing a glance to the silent man before her, might call it what I deserved.

'Did it hurt?'

'Not much.'

'But you didn't die. I'm glad.'

Amused by the solemn little girl and her apparent fixation on the gruesome details of the accident, Lucy smiled and said, 'It was nothing.'

'People do die falling off horses,' the girl replied matter-of-factly. 'My *mamá* did.'

Lucy's horrified intake of breath sounded loud in the silent room.

CHAPTER NINE

'She was dead when *Papá* found her—'

This casual revelation drew another exclamation from an unprepared Lucy before Santiago, his deep voice calm and wiped of any hint of emotion, cut across his daughter.

'Gabby, leave Miss Fitzgerald in peace. You can interrogate her later.'

Lucy's eyes flew to his face. In profile his expression was veiled, nothing other than the suggestion of tension in the muscles along his firm jaw to suggest they were discussing a tragedy.

Tears started in her eyes as an empathic shudder ran through her body...to lose his wife in a senseless accident and to discover her body... A bone-deep chill settled on Lucy as she realised what he must have thought when he found her... *Oh, God, to have it all brought back...and I thought he was overreacting!*

He was a tough man, but even steel had weaknesses.

The horrid realisation that she had been the catalyst for bringing back heaven knew what sort of nightmarish memories made her feel like an utterly selfish... And it was her fault and why...?

She had known it was wrong and she had done it anyway.

'But, *Papá*, I...' The girl met her father's eyes and gave an exaggerated sigh. 'All right, but I was only—'

'Say goodbye to Miss Fitzgerald, Gabriella.'

'Goodbye, Miss Fitzgerald,' she trotted out obediently.

'Goodbye, Gabby.' No mystery why Santiago's parenting skills veered towards the overprotective!

The child threw a half smile at Lucy over her shoulder before she left the room, dragging her feet with exaggerated reluctance.

Lucy half expected him to follow his daughter out, but instead Santiago moved into the room, closing the door behind him.

'Your wife died…' Lucy began awkwardly. 'The circumstances…I didn't know…'

His shoulders lifted. 'There is no reason you should know.'

Subtitles were not required to read the silent addition of *back off*!

'So you are feeling better?' His eyes touched the purple smudges beneath her eyes. 'The lab results on Ramon have confirmed the strain of bug… You have been relatively lucky. They have kept him in to rule out any complications.'

Her eyes widened in alarm. 'Complications?'

'Apparently there have been rare cases when the kidneys are affected. It is only a precaution. The doctor will be here to see you shortly. In the meantime just ring the bell.' He nodded to the old-fashioned arrangement above the bed and Lucy visualised it ringing in the nether regions of the place—she had no intention of using it or of staying in bed.

'In the meantime I am instructed to tell you to take plenty of fluids.'

It would be a brave person who instructed him to do anything. 'That's very…kind of you.' *Kind* was not a word she had ever imagined using in relation to this autocratic man but he had been, and she had not exactly been grateful. 'But totally not necessary. I'm fine. If someone could bring my clothes—' holding back her hair with one hand, she pulled back the covers '—I'll—'

'You're weak as a kitten,' he said, placing a finger on her chest that sent her back against the pillows. Pulling back the bed covers, he leaned in to tuck them around her, affording Lucy a smell of the soap he had used mingled with the warm male smell of him.

'You can't keep me here against my will!'

He nodded his head. 'True, I can't, always assuming of course that I would want to.' His amused glance travelled over her rigid figure, making Lucy painfully aware of how awful she must look... Several steps down from dragged through a hedge was clearly no temptation...not that she wanted to tempt him.

He took a step back and nodded towards the door. 'Feel free to go back to the *finca* if you wish.' Bowing his head, he made a sweeping gesture of invitation.

Suspicious of the easy victory—why the sudden climb down?—she viewed him through narrowed blue eyes and didn't move.

'I'm sure Harriet will drag herself out of her own sickbed to look after you.'

'Harriet!' In the act of tossing her hair back in defiance, Lucy froze, her beautiful features melting into a horrified mask of dismay. She had not given her friend a single thought.

Though tempted to torment her a little more, he soothed, 'Do not worry.' She looked ready to leap out of bed there and then, which would probably result in her collapsing. She looked, he decided, as weak as a day-old chick. 'Harriet is being taken care of. A man is seeing to the animals and a girl from the village is helping out in the house.'

'You did that?'

'Harriet is my tenant. It is my responsibility... Had I

known of her accident I would have arranged for help until she was on her feet.'

'And I wouldn't have come. We would never have met.'

Santiago contemplated the afternoon sun that was pooling on the dark wood beneath his feet and grunted. 'In a perfect world,' he agreed, thinking how much simpler his life had been a few short days ago.

He had said many worse things to her but strangely this hurt more than any of the others. It was not even a rebuke, it was just a rather obvious statement of fact—she had caused him nothing but trouble, had gone out of her way to do so.

'You're crying?' Santiago had always had a cynical attitude to female tears. At best they were irritating, at worst manipulative. His usual response was to walk away or ignore them.

For some reason he found himself able to do neither.

'No!' she said, sounding insulted by the suggestion. 'I'm fine.' She sniffed, sticking out her chin and looking anything but. 'And I'm sorry to have been a nuisance and put everyone to so much trouble.'

He shrugged. 'I think that as my brother poisoned you it was the least we could do.'

Lucy's eyes went wide as she blurted the question that she couldn't get out of her head. 'She wasn't riding Santana, was she?'

Santiago tensed, his body stiffening before he vented a hard laugh. 'Magdalena was afraid of horses.' It turned out that she was more afraid of his bad opinion. 'All horses. She would not have gone into the same stable as Santana. The mare she was on broke a leg in the fall and had to be put down.'

'But if she was afraid—?' She broke off, colouring. 'Sorry, it's none of my—'

'You want to know why my wife was riding if she hated

horses?' His voice was harsh. 'It is a fair question,' he conceded with a tight nod of his dark head. 'She went out riding because I said she should conquer her fears. I told her she should suck it up and stop being pathetic.'

His thoughts flew back to the incident that had preceded the tragedy; over the years he had replayed it innumerable times.

It had been Gabby's birthday. The previous day he had cleared his calendar to be part of the celebrations, cancelled a series of important meetings and had been feeling pretty smug about taking his paternal responsibilities seriously. Apparently he took his husbandly ones, in light of the subsequent events, much less so.

Magdalena was a great organiser and the party had been a big hit for everyone except his daughter, who had spent the day watching wistfully as her friends clambered on the bouncy castle and sat on the back of the placid Shetland pony while it was led around the garden.

When he had asked her if she wanted a turn she had shook her head. 'It's very dangerous. *Mamá* says I might get hurt.'

When he had carried her onto the bouncy castle her terrified sobs had been so pathetic that he'd had to remove her. He had known then that situation could no longer be ignored.

That evening he had confronted Magdalena, too angry to be tactful or gentle, accusing her of infecting their once-fearless daughter with her own insecurities and fears... He had shouted her down when she had protested that it was her duty to protect her child from danger.

'Danger! You think a lollipop represents danger,' he had mocked angrily. 'I will not have our daughter grow up to be a woman who is afraid of her own shadow.'

'A woman like me?'

The silence had stretched—they had had this conversation before, or a version of it, many times, and it was at this point where he rushed in to comfort her, but this time he had held back. He had previously told her everything would be all right and the situation had not improved; if anything it had deteriorated.

So Santiago, still angry with himself as much as her for allowing the situation to continue, had hardened his heart to the appeal in her eyes, ignored her quivering lip and said angrily, 'Yes.'

When they had married Santiago had been convinced that with his support and freed from her parents' oppressive influence his timid wife would blossom. He had seen himself as the noble hero Magdalena had thought him.

His lip curled into a contemptuous smile. He had thought it would be easy but in those days he had imagined that love could conquer all, that he could mould Magdalena into the woman he had known she could be.

In reality the gentle timidity that had originally drawn him to her and aroused his strongly developed protective instincts had begun to irritate him.

In retrospect he could see that his disenchantment had begun after Gabby had been born. He had always believed that a mother should be a strong role model for a daughter, but it had seemed to him that the only things Magdalena was passing on to their child were a lack of confidence and a whole host of phobias.

'She was doing what she thought I wanted,' he told Lucy now. *And you are having this conversation why, Santiago? And with the woman your brother is sleeping with, of all people.* 'Magdalena wanted to please me and it killed her—I killed her.'

And you, she thought, *have been punishing yourself ever since...* This was a side of Santiago Silva that she had never seen. Part of her way of coping with this man was listing him under the heading of inhuman—the suggestion he had normal vulnerabilities made her feel uneasy.

'If that were true you would be in prison,' she offered in a level voice. 'It was a terrible tragic accident,' she added, refusing to offer him the condemnation he appeared to be inviting.

'Accidents cannot be predicted.' And neither, it seemed, could her response—he'd thought he could have relied on her to take advantage of the chink in his armour.

The self-loathing in his voice made her wince. 'What do you want me to say—that it was your fault?'

'I do not wish you to say anything.' She could have legitimately asked why he had introduced the subject, but she didn't. After a quick glance at his face she reached for the crystal water jug, not anticipating the weight of it. Her wrist trembled, sending an ice cube skidding across the polished surface of the bedside table.

With a grunt Santiago took it from her hand, his fingers brushing hers. The contact was light but the response of her nerve endings was anything but... It zigzagged through her body like an internal lightning bolt.

'Let me—you'll have the place drenched.'

She watched from under her lashes, nursing her still-tingling fingers against her chest as he filled her glass with a steady hand.

'You have a lovely daughter,' she said, turning the conversation into a less painful topic. 'She is back home?'

'An extended summer break. My lovely daughter has been excluded from school...again. However I'm sure my daughter's schooling is of no interest to you.' Women who were ruled by self-interest were rarely interested in any subject that did not directly affect them.

Self-interest has her living in a primitive farmhouse, acting as unpaid labour and nursemaid?

Santiago turned a deaf ear to the contribution of his objective self. He hadn't figured out what her endgame was yet, but he was confident that it would in time become clear just what lay behind this apparently altruistic act of helping out a friend.

The blue eyes turned to him were not uninterested; they had softened with what appeared genuine sympathy. 'She's unhappy?'

His jaw tightened in response to the combination of the probing question and the overflow of empathy aimed his way. This was the reason he did not open up, not even to his own family. After Magdalena died there had been far too many who had viewed him as a tortured soul they could save—it was not a role he had any intention of adopting.

'She is spoilt.' His tone signalled the subject was closed. The message was not ambiguous, but Lucy either didn't pick up on it or chose not to.

'Perhaps she doesn't like school…?' Even as she made tentative suggestion she was anticipating a frigid 'mind your own business' response—it didn't come.

'Like? Life requires we do things we do not like.'

Did she not think that he didn't want to protect his child from everything in life that could hurt her? Following his instincts would not prepare her for what life would throw at her. Of course he was concerned that he had the balance wrong, that he was going too far, being too tough…

Habits, he brooded darkly, were notoriously hard to break and he had spent the early years playing the bad-cop parent to Magdalena's good cop in an effort to achieve some sort of balance.

His frustration found release in his snarling addition.

'Duty may be an alien concept to you…'

Lucy let go of the pillow she was clutching in front of her as an energising flash of anger brought her bolt upright in bed. 'Yes, well, let's just pretend for the moment that I have a vague idea of what it means.'

'I hated school also, but a person does not run away from things they hate… It is habit forming.' And Santiago was not about to allow his daughter to develop this habit.

Lucy was unimpressed by the logic. 'Is that from the same book that says what doesn't kill you makes you stronger? Has it occurred to you to ask her why she runs away?'

He slung her an impatient look. Did the woman think he was stupid? 'Of course I have asked her.' He gritted his teeth and delivered a white clenched smile. 'And I find myself reluctant to take advice on parenting from someone who is hardly a role model for any young woman.'

Lucy's expression froze over. 'Well, I'll try not to infect her with my…' She stopped and took a steadying breath. 'I'm sorry to have put you to so much trouble,' she added with frigid formality. 'Not you personally, obviously, but your staff. Everyone has been very kind.'

'As I told you—it was the least we could do.' Actually the least would have been not fighting with her while she was whacked with exhaustion and ill.

That silent addendum was pretty implicit in her blue eyes.

And it was true, Santiago acknowledged. He had felt her getting close and the irony was he knew he only had himself to blame. He had opened the door and invited her to stamp around in her size fives in his head and then he had reacted instinctively to push her away as hard and brutally as possible.

'How is Ramon?'

'I'm visiting him this afternoon,' he told her coldly.

'Will you give him my love?'

Santiago's face was a mask of contempt as he looked down at her and snarled, 'No, I will not!'

She recoiled from the anger in his reply. 'Fine, I'll do it

myself when I get out of here and don't worry—it will take an earthquake to keep me here a second longer than necessary!' she yelled after his retreating back.

CHAPTER TEN

WHEN the doctor called a few minutes later Lucy was feeling so wretched that she was not surprised when he said that the bug she had contracted was a particularly virulent strain. In fact, she almost retorted—yes, the Santini Strain!

Lucy, who had been hoping for permission to leave, was dismayed when he announced he wanted her to stay in bed until the next day and after that he would review the situation.

In the event, she did not feel much like getting out of bed. She slept a good deal of the time, waking on one occasion during the early evening to find Gabby perched on the end of her bed.

She knew that Santiago would be furious if he found her there and, as the girl began with, 'Don't worry, *Papá* has gone to the hospital to see Uncle Ramon,' it was pretty obvious that the child had been warned not to visit.

She was saved from having to shoo the child away by the arrival of Josef, who came with one of the rehydration drinks that the doctor had instructed she take through the evening.

He left taking a reluctant Gabby with him.

The next morning Lucy was feeling better and would have welcomed a visit from Gabby to stop her replaying every conversation she had ever had with Santiago in her head over and over. She had improved on many of her responses and never made others.

When he arrived she was able to assure the doctor that she had spent a comfortable night; there were some things you didn't tell anyone, even your doctor, and the dreams that she had woken from hot, sweaty and shaking the previous night came under that heading!

After a medical twenty questions he pronounced himself happy for her to go home if she managed a light lunch with no ill effects.

Lucy would have loved to have explored the fascinating building, but she reluctantly passed on the opportunity, keeping to her room to avoid the possibility of running into Santiago, and he did not seek her out—not that she had expected him to. He might have been avoiding her, but it was equally likely that he had forgotten she was there. With this self-pitying reflection she made herself consume a portion of the light lunch that was served on a silver tray.

Another night in this place was not an option.

'I feel so bad about Lucy.'

His brother looked like death warmed up and in deference to his weakened condition he had not brought up the subject uppermost in his mind, but now that Ramon himself had introduced it Santiago found himself unable to hold back.

'For God's sake, Ramon, I know you're bewitched by the woman and I admit she is…compelling…but—'

Ramon waved the hand attached to an intravenous drip. 'But I'm not sleeping with her.'

He saw his brother's expression of disbelief and gave a weak smile.

'Oh, don't get me wrong, I would if I could, or rather if *she* would. She isn't interested in me. I found out about you warning her off and I… The truth is I'm fed up of you trying to run my life. For God's sake, Santiago, how am I meant to learn from my mistakes if you never let me make any?

'I knew you'd got it into your head that poor Lucy is some sort of dangerous femme fatale and I wanted to...' he took a deep breath, there were some advantages to being at death's door—his brother couldn't hit him '...teach you a lesson.' He waited for a reaction and when there wasn't one added crankily, 'For God's sake, say something. I'm dying here.'

'You're not sleeping with her?' If Ramon was not, then he... Santiago's chest swelled as he released a deep sigh. 'Good.'

'That's it—good?'

Santiago's lips curved into a slow smile as he bared his white teeth and confirmed softly, 'Very good.'

Very good that he no longer had to feel jealous of his own brother. That he no longer had to rationalise his determination to keep Ramon out of Lucy's bed and finally that he no longer had to pretend that Lucy's bed wasn't exactly where he, Santiago, wanted to be.

What was not good about the anticipation of enjoying sex with a beautiful, experienced woman? He would satisfy this hunger and get Lucy Fitzgerald out of his system.

A few hours later, staying that extra night was looking like a real possibility. Drumming her fingers on the table top in the small salon she had been seated in to wait for transport, Lucy glanced at her watch.

She was deciding to give it half an hour before she took matters into her own hands and called a taxi when the door opened. She half rose and then sat down heavily, the eager expression on her face fading to one of almost comic horror.

'I didn't expect to see you still here.' Santiago stood there looking down, arrogance and hauteur etched in every angle and plane of his incredible face. 'I thought nothing short of

a natural disaster would keep you here a second longer...'
That and Josef, who could always be relied on to rise to the
occasion. The man, he decided, deserved a raise. He'd said
do not let her leave but Josef was more subtle.

Lucy flushed and got to her feet. 'I'm still waiting for the
car,' she explained in a small stiff voice. 'Josef said it won't
be long.' That had been two hours ago.

He elevated a sardonic brow.

'I'm sorry if I've overstayed my welcome...' She walked
towards the door, back ramrod stiff.

'Sit down.' He sighed.

Responding to the pressure of the hand on her shoulder,
Lucy sank back down into her seat, her breathing coming
quicker as she combated the electrical tingle caused by the
light contact.

His eyes brushed her face and for a brief moment she saw
something in his dark hooded stare that made her stomach
lurch, then it was gone—if it had ever been there...? Lucy
had started to mistrust her own senses when she was around
him.

She concentrated on not panting—pretty much a give-
away as he walked across the room to the bureau, pulling
the heavy stopper off a decanter sitting there. He poured a
finger of the liquid into a glass and proceeded to toss it off
in one swallow, then he reached for the decanter again.

He refilled it before looking directly at her. 'Is that what
I said?'

'No,' she conceded, noticing that he looked relaxed...yet
those tensed bunched muscles in his neck told a different
story. 'But—'

'Are you this defensive and prickly with everyone or is it
just me?' He ground the words from between clenched teeth
as he covered the bottom of another glass. 'Do you think I
am not capable of saying what I mean?'

She thought of saying she didn't drink spirits, but decided the stuff might be of some medicinal benefit so after a pause she took the glass he held out to her. She nodded graciously before she held it to her nose and breathed in the fragrance.

'I'm sure you're totally capable of...' She stopped, losing her train of thought as her gaze met his. A comment from a deeply in lust acquaintance popped into her head: 'God, I can't look at him without thinking how incredible he'd be in bed.'

At the time Lucy had struggled to imagine what that would be like.

'I'm...cautious with people,' she blurted, drawing his curious stare to her face.

She lowered her eyes but continued to watch him over the rim of the glass, thinking, *Not cautious enough with you.*

She should, she realised, have run in the opposite direction the moment she saw this man. Instead she had spent her time inventing reasons to be around him, telling herself she was a victim of circumstance, when in reality she had been a victim of her libido.

So just add me to the list of women that have made fools of themselves to catch the eye of Santiago.

Cautious struck him as an interesting choice of word and one that he would never have applied to someone who seemed to act first, think later.

She had lectured him on parenting, stolen a valuable horse without thinking and now, it turned out, been part of a conspiracy to teach him a lesson. 'So I'm not special.'

If only, she thought as he shrugged off his jacket and draped it around the back of a chair. His innate elegance as always sent a shimmy of sensation down her spine. Her fascination with him—with everything about him—showed no sign of diminishing. If anything it became stronger. He was like an addictive drug in her bloodstream. *Look but don't inhale, Lucy,* she told herself, *and never, ever touch!*

Lucy followed him with her eyes while he loosed the tie he wore around his neck; she had never imagined she could get pleasure just from looking at a man.

'I was just catching up with my emails,' she said, nodding to the machine on the table, adding, 'Josef said it would be all right. Harriet doesn't have internet access, and I was hoping to see you,' she lied.

'I'm flattered.' He selected a chair, pulled it a little closer to her and lowered his long lean frame into it with another display of riveting fluid grace.

'I was hoping you had news of Ramon.' As their eyes met Lucy had the horrid feeling he could see right through her lie; she felt terrible because she actually hadn't thought of Ramon once this evening.

'Second best again.' He sighed. 'You know how to put a man in his place.'

The prospect of becoming Lucy's lover excited him as nothing had in a very long time. She challenged him and not just with her incredible looks. She was the most stunningly beautiful creature he had ever seen, but he had discovered that Lucy had an intellect to match her beauty. All that and the woman ate him up with her hungry eyes… She literally trembled with lust when their hands brushed. All the bloody restraint he had been displaying was killing him.

His concentration was shot to hell; he couldn't focus on anything; in short he had lost his edge and the cure for his problems was within tantalising reach. He blinked to clear the image of her, magnificent and naked, straddling him, flashing through his head. Lost his edge…? Hell, at times it felt as if he had lost his mind!

While she was obviously not the two-dimensional scarlet woman the media had painted her, she clearly had a past, but then who didn't? He did not require every woman he took to bed to be a blameless virgin. In fact had such a female existed such attributes would have immediately put her off-limits, not to mention bored him senseless.

The last thing Santiago was looking for at this stage in his life was a woman who had been waiting for the 'right man'; he was nobody's right man.

He had tried denying the existence of this strong attraction—it hadn't worked. He had tried waiting for it to pass—it hadn't. That just left working through it…the third was by far the most attractive option.

'I've had an interesting conversation with Ramon.'

Lucy tensed at the seemingly casual comment. Her guilty conscience was making her jumpy—if Ramon had come clean about their fake romance, Santiago would have come in here breathing fire and retribution.

The knowledge made her relax slightly.

'How is he?' she asked, matching his casual tone as she sat back in her seat, leaning her elbows on the wooden arms of the chair.

'They are discharging him at the weekend.'

Her relief was genuine. 'Great!'

'So you can take up where you left off with the big romance.'

'I wouldn't call it a big romance…exactly…' she muttered, dodging his gaze and taking another gulp of the brandy—too much too fast. She choked as it hit the back of her throat and settled in a warm glow in the pit of her stomach.

'No? What would you call it?'

'It's hard to say,' she admitted, sidestepping the issue.

Santiago laced his fingers and, resting his chin on the bridge they made, smiled at her. 'Try.' His voice was not smiling; neither were the eyes fixed like lasers on her face.

She slung him an irritated glance, compressed her lips and

crossed one ankle over the other. 'We're not in a long-term relationship, all right?' she snapped without looking at him.

'And have you ever been—with anyone?'

'The odds are not exactly stacked in favour of lasting relationships, are they?' The sad fact did not stop her being a ridiculous optimist and believing that there was someone out there for everyone, just sometimes they missed one another.

The reply would only have displeased a man who was looking for long term and he wasn't. 'So you are not looking for anything permanent.' All good, he told himself.

Show me a woman who says she isn't and I'll show you a liar, she thought. 'Permanent requires making concessions and I'm not good at that.'

'So you don't believe that there is someone out there who will complete you…a soul mate…?'

Was that what his pretty wife had been, his soul mate?

Lucy lifted her gaze, bright smile in place the moment their eyes meshed. Her smile guttered as she searched his face and her eyes widened.

'You know.'

'Know what?'

The display of fake ignorance drew a growl from Lucy.

'Ah,' he drawled. 'You are referring to the fact you haven't actually slept with my brother, that there is no steamy affair.'

In retrospect Santiago could see that he should have guessed the truth sooner, and would have had his judgement not been clouded by sexual jealousy. He had watched them together, seen them flirt and fought a desire to rip them apart. If he'd been thinking straight he might have seen past the window dressing to the lack of chemistry.

Her chin went up. 'Not yet.'

'Not ever!'

He acted with bewildering speed and zero warning. One minute he was lounging in the chair several safe feet away, the next he was right there, pulling her out of her chair and drawing her body up against his hard, lean front.

She opened her mouth to ask him what the hell he thought he was doing when he took her face between his big hands, framing it with his fingers, resting his thumbs in the angle of her jaw as he tipped her face up to his.

The rampant wild hunger in his glowing eyes drew a raw whimper from her aching throat.

His eyes were like a dark flame as they moved across her face. 'You're so beautiful.' His powerful chest lifted in a silent sigh as he shook his head in an attitude of disbelief. 'I keep looking for a flaw but there isn't one.'

Lucy trembled, weak with lust and longing as she stared up at him with passion-glazed drowning blue eyes. 'What is happening?' she whispered.

'I think you know.'

Her stomach quivered and clenched as his long fingers speared deep into the single skein of her hair, lifting it off her neck to expose the smooth lines of her throat.

Her head went back as his warm lips nuzzled the wildly beating blue-veined pulse spot at the base of her throat. The moist contact sent a fresh slug of frantic desire shuddering through her trembling body.

Her even white teeth clamped along the quivering curve of her full lower lip and her heavy lids drifted closed as he moved up her throat, his lips barely touching her skin, the light contact blitzing a tingling, erotic trail of sensation.

His lips brushed her cheekbone, her ear, then, lifting his head, he touched the cushiony softness of her full lower lip, dragging his thumb across the outline before he bent his head. Slowly he fitted his mouth to hers, but when the kiss came it was not slow, it exploded, searing, not gentle, but rough, raw and hungry. Swept away on a swirling tide of elemental need, she reached up her arms, circling his neck as she met the darting intrusion of his tongue with her own, the taste of him exciting her unbearably.

As they kissed his hands were on her body, sliding down her spine, cupping her bottom, pulling her up and against the rock-hard bold imprint of his erection.

'You've been waiting for this.'

She looked into the silver lights shining in his dark eyes and felt dizzy. 'Yes,' she admitted, thinking, *I've been waiting for you.*

Nostrils flared, he breathed in the scent of her hair. 'I want to wrap myself in this,' he said, letting the pale strands slip through his fingers. 'I want to be inside you.'

The throaty admission sent a jolt of sexual longing through her body and the need inside her rose until she could barely breathe, think… 'Take me to bed, Santiago?' she whispered, simultaneously shocked and excited by her own boldness. 'Please.'

The febrile glitter of passion in his dark eyes made her tremble while for several heart-stopping moments he searched her face, then nodded. Taking her hand, he walked towards the bookcase, then, pressing a hand to a panel, stood to one side as a large section swung open.

'A secret door!' she gasped.

'Hardly a secret, but it is useful.'

Lucy entered the secret space and found herself, not in a traditional dark and gloomy room but surrounded by limestone walls that gleamed in the electric light that shone from sconces. All the way up the spiral stone staircase a heavy red rope strung to the wall provided handholds.

How many women had he taken up these stairs? Lucy wondered as she began to climb the stone spiral staircase concealed inside the wall, the growing sense of anticipation making her heart beat hard.

She shook her head and pushed the thought away. Forget

the others—this was her night. At the top Santiago reached over her shoulder and pressed a panel, the door this end opened into a massive panelled room.

'My bedroom,' he said, watching her face. 'And my bed,' he added.

His dark intense gaze didn't leave her face for one second as he led her across to the carved oak bed that took pride of place. He peeled back the plain white bedlinen and deposited Lucy on the bed.

Not sure she'd ever get used to being picked up as though she were small and fragile, Lucy pulled herself up on her knees, swaying as the mattress beneath her moved.

She pushed her hair from her eyes and looked at him. 'Santiago…?'

He responded with a grunt of acknowledgement and continued to strip off his clothes.

'I need to say something.' Need, not want. Nobody on the brink of having sex with— 'Oh, God!' she gasped as he fought his way successfully out of his shirt, having sent the buttons scattering noisily across the floor.

There was not an ounce of surplus flesh on his hard body to hide the perfect muscle definition. Every individual muscle in his torso was perfectly delineated beneath his satiny gold skin.

Moist heat flashed between her thighs, but she felt a tremor of fear. He was magnificent. Certainly not the sort of person to whom you wanted to admit: 'I'm not great in bed but I'll do my best.'

'Look, I'm not…there's something you should know about me—'

This time the distraction was even more severe. Having kicked away his trousers, he was walking to the bed wearing just a pair of boxers that were totally inadequate to disguise the level of his arousal.

A pulse of sexual longing slammed through her body.

'We have all done things we are not proud of.'

Oh, God, he obviously thought the thing she wanted to get off her chest was more along the lines of 'my night of passion with a football team', not 'I'm actually a clueless virgin'.

He arranged himself beside her, long, sleek and incredible, and slid his hand inside her shirt. 'No, really—' The rest of her protest was lost in his mouth, then a second later gone…as his tongue stabbed deep into her mouth and she thought, *I can do this!*

It felt natural…easy and wildly exciting to kiss him back, touch his skin, taste… 'Oh, God, I want to taste you.' Fascinated by the fluid-looking ripple of muscle under his satiny skin, she reached out, spreading her fingers across the ridges of his flat belly, and felt him gasp.

'Dios Mio!' he groaned, tipping her onto her back and almost simultaneously slipping the buttons on her blouse with dexterity that suggested a lot of practice.

Just as well one of us has, said the practical voice in her head.

'You will,' he promised throatily. He buried his face between the soft swell of her warm breasts, pressing them together as he slid the straps down her shoulders, peeling back the lace cups to expose the rosy peaks of her breasts.

When he applied his tongue to first one rigid nipple and then the next, Lucy pushed her head deep into the pillows, exposing the long line of her white neck as she let out a low keening cry.

Her reaction drew a deep masculine growl of appreciation from his throat. *Madre di Dios*, she was so exquisitely sensitive!

One hand resting on her rapidly rising ribcage, he removed her bra completely, freeing up her magnificent breasts. The visual impact brought flashes of colour to the high contours of his cheekbones.

His hands were shaking as he removed her skirt and finally the little lace pants underneath. While he did so he was conscious of her passion-darkened eyes watching him from under her half-closed eyelids; the sexual tension crackling in the air around them was explosive.

A muscle in his lean cheek clenched as his hot glance slid over her silky pale curves. She was the epitome of all things feminine, there was not a sharp angle in her lovely body.

'You are a goddess,' he breathed.

Lucy shook her head. She did not want to be a goddess—they got put on pedestals. She wanted to be held and touched.

'No, I'm a woman.' *Your woman*, she said silently in her head.

The first skin-to-skin contact was overwhelming, a total sensory overload. Her hand slid to the tight curve of his buttock, hard under the boxer shorts he still wore.

Taking her hands captive, he rolled her onto her back and, pinioning them lightly, he knelt over her.

He released her hands as he moved down her body, touching her with his fingers and lips and tongue until all her skin was burning and tingling. She had no idea how long this sweet torment went on, but he seemed to know exactly where and how to touch her, to bring her to a point where there was only Santiago and mindless pleasure. The two were the same in her head.

'This is so...' She writhed, her head flung back, her arms curved above her head as he kissed his way damply down her stomach, still caressing her aching breasts as he moved lower. The hot, liquid throbbing ache between her legs had become almost unbearable when she felt his fingers slide along the silky skin of her inner thigh. She stiffened and felt rather than saw his questioning gaze.

'Is something wrong?'

Heart thumping a wild tattoo that vibrated through her body, she opened her eyes, her greedy gaze sliding over the gleaming muscled contours of his sleek, powerful body.

She looked at him and thought, *Nothing at all. I want this...* She had never wanted anything more than she wanted this...him...now.

In reply she shifted slightly and let her thighs part.

The symbolic invitation wrenched a low feral moan from his throat as he slid the shorts down over his hips.

Her awed gasp of, 'Oh, my goodness!' drew a fierce grin from Santiago, who kicked away the shorts.

Holding her eyes, he took her hand and curved her fingers around the satiny hard column of his erection.

Her blue eyes flew wide then as her fingers tightened. Heat spread through her body and she closed her eyes to intensify the tactile sensation.

'Enough!' Primitive hunger burning through his blood, Santiago took her hand in his and touched her, sliding his fingers across the engorged nub. Her wild cries of delirious pleasure deepened the level of his arousal.

Unable to resist the primitive fire burning in his blood, he could no longer fight the need to bury himself inside her, to feel her tightness around him.

Kissing her, he settled over her, nudging her thighs farther apart with his knee as he slid between them.

'Look at me.'

Lucy was looking at him when he drove deep into her.

She was too involved with what was happening to her own body, the incredible sensation of being filled and stretched, to register his hoarse cry of surprise.

She responded instinctively to the slow erotic movement of his body, rising to meet him, pulling him deeper, wrapping her long legs around him to hold him close to her core, sinking into herself with him.

The sensations were incredible, the pleasure so intense, so sweet, that it brought tears to her eyes. They slipped unchecked down her cheeks.

Swept along on a wave of sensation that was both exhilarating and terrifying in its intensity, she hung onto him, loving his weight pressing her down, loving his hardness filling her—loving him!

'Let go, let go...*querida*,' he urged between the kisses he pressed on her parted lips.

Lucy nodded in agreement even though she had no idea what he meant, then she did.

It felt like falling weightless through space. She had no control over the intense pulses of wild pleasure that spread out through her body like golden arrows; she just gave herself up to them and let it happen.

She was in the centre of this firestorm of hot sensation when she felt his hot pulsing release inside her.

CHAPTER ELEVEN

'THIS isn't possible?' Though his skin was still hot and slick with sweat Santiago's face was very pale as he rolled away.

Not willing to lose the skin-to-skin contact so soon, Lucy looped her thigh across his hip and scooted in closer until they lay side by side again. She lay her head against his hair-roughened chest, running her finger around the flat, pebble hardness of a male nipple.

Lucy lifted her head in protest as he caught her hand and pressed it into the pillow.

'Lucy, will you stop that? I'm trying to…' He stopped. She looked like a lovely wanton angel lying there. How the hell was it possible that he had been her first lover…? A frown pleating his brow, he tried to join the mental dots but no matter which route he took nothing became clearer.

'You're trying to what? Work out why someone took out an injunction to stop a blackmailing bitch selling her sordid kiss-and-tell story when the bitch in question was a clue-less virgin?'

The muscles along his jaw tightened as Santiago ran his hand down her smooth thigh, dragging her in closer. 'Do not use that word.'

'Which one—bitch or virgin?' He did not smile back. 'All right, it isn't complicated, but it is long. I won't bore you with the details.'

'Bore me.'

His tone did not invite debate so she took a deep breath and launched reluctantly into her explanation.

'I did a charity catwalk show and I was introduced to Denis Mulville. He was an advertising executive working for one of the sponsors.

'Long story short, he made me an offer that he thought I couldn't refuse—I did.' She gave a shudder. The man with his horrible wet mouth, fake smile and fake tan had turned her stomach, but she had not realised at that time that he was dangerous.

'He was persistent, flowers and gifts, et cetera, but I sent them back and ignored him, assuming at first that he'd lose interest. Then things got a bit nasty—nobody says no to Denis Mulville apparently.' She felt the tension in Santiago's body and lifted her head. 'Nothing physical, just texts, emails, that sort of thing. Not threats, just suggestions—it was all quite subtle, not nice.'

Santiago, who had struggled to control his feelings while she had laid bare the bones of a story that made his blood boil, swore savagely under his breath. Not nice, a classic example of British understatement, but he was not British and there was nothing understated about the murderous rage hardening inside him.

'The man stalked you,' he said flatly. 'How was it the injunction was against you?' The world had condemned her and he had been only too eager to jump on the bandwagon taking her guilt as a given. He sucked in a deep breath, self-disgust tightening like a fist in the pit of his belly as he thought of the things he had said.

'His final revenge. I wouldn't sleep with him so he invented an affair, confided in friends—actually it seemed everyone knew about it except me. He laid the groundwork so when he claimed later that I was trying to blackmail him he was believed.'

Santiago swore. 'What happened to innocent until proved guilty?'

You did not, he told himself, have to care about a person to care about an injustice—and caring had nothing to do with admiration or respect. After all, how could you not respect someone who had risen above something that would have destroyed many? And she had done so with incredible dignity, not lowering herself even once to the level of the creep who had tried to destroy her.

'This wasn't a trial, it was an injunction. The same rules do not apply,' she told him quietly.

'Madre di Dios!' he grated, burying his face in her fragrant hair as he pulled her into his arms, dragging her body across his.

Lucy sighed as she pushed her face into the angle between his shoulder and chin.

'His identity was protected but not mine—my name was out there, and the best bit was I wasn't allowed to say a word… It was a total gagging order. I couldn't defend myself against anything they decided to write about me.' She rolled onto her back and grabbed a pillow, hugging it to her chest as though it would protect her from the memories.

As he listened to her relate the story in that flat little voice Santiago felt the tightness in his chest increase to the point where he could barely breathe past the outrage he was experiencing. How could she seem so calm, so lacking in bitterness after what had happened to her?

'But the same order protected his name, though of course everyone knew. You've got to hand it to him—it was the perfect revenge…almost poetic when you think about it. Now if I'd really been thinking on my feet I'd have told him I was gay.'

Santiago was not fooled by her laugh. 'He did this because you refused to go to bed with him.'

'Like I said, poetic.'

'Poetic it is…the man is…' He snarled a savage oath and said a word that was not in Lucy's vocabulary, one she was guessing she would not find in many dictionaries, either.

'He's petty and vindictive and not actually worth wasting my life thinking about.' Lucy had lost count of the number of times she had told herself this.

'But when the injunction was lifted…? You were free to speak then…?' This aspect puzzled him. Why hadn't she shot the bastard down in flames when the opportunity came to expose him to the world for what he was?

If it had been him he would have served up justice with a smile on his face and a figurative sword in his hand. Never mind a pound of flesh, Santiago would have claimed the whole worthless carcass!

Lucy tilted her head in acknowledgement as she pushed the pillow under her head. 'Oh, sure, I could have made a fortune with my story.' Despite her joking tone she had received offers. The mocking smile curving her lips vanished as she added sombrely, 'What would have been the point of resurrecting it?'

The dull thud pounding like a metronome in his temples, grappling with the information, the knowledge of what she had been through and come out smiling the other end…he felt a fresh stab of shame when he thought of how he had judged her… How many other people had done the same?

'Besides, everyone that mattered already knew I'd done nothing wrong. My family were great. They stood by me. I know it was hard for them reading that stuff about me, especially since Dad and I hadn't talked in three years, but when—'

'You were estranged from your father? I thought that the Fitzgeralds were tight.'

'We are but that doesn't mean we don't have our fallings out. Dad had plans for me but I wanted something different. With Dad there was only one way and that was his so...'

'He threw you out?' Santiago frowned. As a father he could never imagine a situation where he would deliver an ultimatum that would run the risk of him losing his daughter.

She nodded, seeming to him remarkably philosophical about the past.

'That's why I was modelling to begin with. My dad brought his kids up to be independent and strong, or that's his version of it.'

'Not your version?'

The question drew a rueful laugh from Lucy. 'No, more yours. I sometimes struggled to conform.' And frequently failed completely.

His dark brows hit his hairline. 'You're suggesting I'm like your father...?'

The startled offence in his voice dragged a laugh from Lucy. She ran a hand down his muscled flank and pressed a kiss against the centre of his hair-roughened chest.

Santiago's mind struggled to stay on track as his lust stirred into life.

'I suppose you have as much in common as powerful men with principles do.'

'So you think I have the odd principle.'

'You're not all bad,' she admitted huskily.

'So what was your father's version of strong?'

'Never admitting you're wrong even to yourself...oh, and tears are definitely out, and, well, actually I think his method of teaching his children to swim about sums up his attitude to parenting.'

Santiago's brows lifted. He knew the man by reputation obviously, but… 'Not seriously…?'

'Yep, he threw us in the deep end of the pool and we either sank or swum.' Santiago looked shocked so, anxious to dispel any impression that her father had been a monster, she added hastily, 'Not that he'd have let us actually drown. He threw us a lifeline if necessary.'

'And was it necessary with you?' He found himself seeing her as a kid trying to please her father, trying to keep up with her older siblings.

'No, I got to the side, after a fashion.'

'And what doesn't kill you makes you stronger…?'

The reminder of her earlier comment made Lucy grimace and grin.

'Or in your case fearless.'

Lucy heard the grudging admiration in his voice and thought, *If only you knew.* If he got to know the real Lucy he would be very disappointed, but no problem because he wouldn't.

'I get scared,' she admitted.

'When were you scared?'

'I was scared stiff of being awful in bed.' This was weird—after years of successfully boxing up her feelings she was leaking information like a sieve.

He ran a finger down the curve of her cheek and felt her tremble. His lips curved upwards into a smile that left his eyes dark and burning. 'You weren't.'

She lowered her eyes, suddenly feeling shy, which was crazy after what they had just shared.

'I get that after the Mulville guy you might have been wary of getting involved, but before surely there were boys… men?' It still made no sense to him that a woman who was so sensual should come to his bed a virgin.

'I dated when I was young but my dad scared them off.'

'The idea of Gabby bringing home boys brings me out in a cold sweat.'

She laughed and tossed a pillow at his head. 'You want to start worrying when she doesn't bring them home.'

He grinned back, looking so handsome that her heart flipped and skipped a beat. 'You have a point.'

'So didn't you have men queuing round the block when you were a model?' His dark glance made a leisurely journey from her soft lips to her full, firm breasts and back. He swallowed. 'I find that very hard to believe.'

'Actually you'd be surprised, but, sure, I dated a little. The thing was, it usually turned out that the guy wanted a trophy girlfriend to parade in front of his mates and I didn't fancy being anyone's arm candy. In my experience the nice guys assume you are unattainable when you're a model or brainless. I once thought of seeing...' She flushed a little as her eyes fell from his. 'But I chickened out. It all seemed so... clinical. That probably sounds stupid to you.'

Santiago thought of the woman he had shared a bed with this time last year and could not remember her face; she probably couldn't remember his. For a moment he almost envied Lucy. 'No, not stupid.' Just untarnished and idealistic—the sort of woman who could be hurt... He pushed away the thought.

There had been no coercion. She had wanted this as much as he had...so why couldn't he shift the vague sense of guilt?

'Besides, it was no problem.' She had simply assumed she was not highly sexed. 'Probably because I didn't know what I was missing.' Now she did, but it remained hard to imagine doing what she had with Santiago with any other man.

'And now you do.'

Lucy nodded, her eyes darkened to midnight-blue as she gazed into his face... The emotional ache of longing in her throat increased as she greedily absorbed the strong lines and planes of his proud patrician features.

'I've never been anyone's first before...' Cool and spiky on the outside and smouldering and sensual on the inside. The idea of being her second, third and fourth pretty much consumed him. He had never experienced the sort of rampant, relentless hunger he felt when he looked at Lucy in his life before. It was a chemical reaction, quite arbitrary, but it was easy to see why people who found themselves in the grip of such relentless passion mistook these feelings of lust for love.

Happily he was not in danger of making this mistake.

'Well, I'm glad you were mine—you made it very good for me.'

'We do seem...compatible...?'

Lucy nodded and wondered where this was going.

'You are here for a while?' She tipped her head. 'There is no reason that we should not continue to be compatible?'

'Sex, you mean?' How did that work—did they compare diaries? The cold-blooded approach made her uneasy. Casual sex had never really appealed to her, but she was not about to knock back the chance of having Santiago show her what she'd been missing. She was totally hooked and deeply in lust with him.

'You are looking for more?'

Despite the wariness she saw in his eyes, she resisted the temptation to say what she knew he wanted to hear, what a girl in her position was meant to say. Instead she responded with as much honesty as possible—total honesty would have meant admitting she would take anything he was willing to give, but she still had a modicum of pride.

'I don't know what I'm looking for, but I suppose that after this...' Her glance slid to the tumbled bedclothes as, unable to keep the wistfulness from her voice—what woman did not want to be wooed?—she added with a laugh, 'Dates

and flowers would be kind of...' she felt his eyes on her
face and shrugged '...not exactly required with someone as
easy as me.'

His lips thinned in displeasure. 'I would not call you easy,
Lucy. And I do not date, and for the record I have not given
any woman flowers since my wife died.' The thought brought
a familiar stab of guilt; flowers could not compensate for a
total selfish lack of interest in a person.

Her amazed violet-blue eyes flew to his face. 'You mean
you haven't done...this since— God, no, of course not,' she
muttered, breaking off in embarrassed confusion.

For some inexplicable reason she kept blurting the first
thought that came into her head, no matter how foolish...and
it didn't get any more foolish than the suggestion of Santiago
Silva living the life of a monk!

He looked faintly amused. 'No, I have not been celibate,
that is not in my nature. I have had lovers but none who require or expect dates or flowers.'

Again before the thought was fully formed it leapt from
her lips. 'You don't mean you sleep with...?' She stopped,
this time blushing vividly.

Reaching out to touch the curve of her cheek, he felt her
shiver. A woman had never responded to him the way she
did. Smiling, he shook his head. 'Sleep with...' He stopped,
a look of startled realisation spreading across his face as he
caught her drift.

His hand fell away. 'I have never had to pay for sex, Lucy,'
he said, not sure if he was insulted or amused by her comment.

'I'm not saying you would have to—obviously you could
have anyone you wanted.'

Right now he wanted her—right now.

'I just thought you might...I read this story once when
after the hero's girlfriend died he only slept with prostitutes

because that way he didn't think he was being unfaithful to her memory…and I'm babbling, aren't I?'

Her comments had inadvertently made him think of the expensive parting gifts his secretary gift-wrapped at the end of a relationship, gifts that had not been unappreciated even though the recipients, women successful in their own right, had all been more than capable of buying their own jewels.

Did Lucy have a point?

'I am not looking for anything permanent, Lucy.'

Her eyes widened. 'God, no, of course not. I never thought that…you…I…that this was…'

'Come here and I will show you what I mean.'

There was nothing even faintly cold about the smouldering glow in his eyes. Lucy stopped talking with relief and gazed at him. 'Oh, yes, please!'

A week later there had been no diary comparing but a lot of sex, although the previous night had been the first time she had stayed over. Not because he had asked her to stay but because she had fallen asleep and woken at five.

It had taken all her willpower to resist Santiago's very persuasive argument to stay longer, but she had and he had not looked at all happy when she had dragged on her clothes and rushed back to the *finca*, dropping a hasty kiss on his lean cheek as she'd left.

She wasn't sure why it seemed so important to her for Harriet not to know she had spent the night; it wasn't as if she were ashamed. After all, having casual sex was not a crime and the older woman was no prude. And Harriet had to have known something was going on with Santiago because, it didn't matter how discreet you were, in a small community like this there were no secrets.

Even so the older woman had not brought up the subject. Perhaps she'd been waiting for her to do so? Lucy mused.

But what was she meant to say? She was not in a committed relationship. She could not talk about Santiago and say 'we'; they were not a couple. She had assumed that they were exclusive for the duration of the affair but it had not, she realised, been spelt out.

Should she bring up the subject? she wondered as she walked across the yard to the stable block. The idea of Santiago even thinking about other women while he was with her made her feel sick to the stomach... The thought that he could be with another woman and then come to her... Hand extended towards the stable door, she froze and closed her eyes, shuddering through a wave of intense nausea as her hand closed into a white-knuckled fist that left the imprint of her neatly trimmed nails in the skin of her palm.

The nausea was real; happily the knife she felt plunging in her chest was not...though, God, did it hurt! Lucy lifted her chin. She hardly recognised the emotions she was feeling... Hell, she hardly recognised herself. She took a deep breath and stepped into the shadowy coolness of the stable. She would, she decided, bring the subject up when she saw him.

The intention was forgotten the moment she heard the plaintive cry. She ran down to the end stall. The animal lying there in some distress bore little resemblance to the one some sixth sense had made her fetch in the previous evening from the pasture. Though she was not due, the heavily pregnant jenny had obviously gone into labour early and even to Lucy's inexpert eye it looked as if things were not going well.

Lucy dropped down beside the animal, making soothing noises and feeling totally useless as she made a cursory examination of the animal before she ran back into the house to ring for the vet. She struggled to maintain her calm in the face of the reply she received from the man's wife.

'So when are you expecting him back?'

Lucy, tapping her feet impatiently, gritted her teeth when

the answer proved frustratingly vague. Explaining the situation again, she asked that the vet call back as soon as possible.

'Whenever that might be,' she muttered to herself as she set the receiver down. Her hand lifted to her hair, sliding her fingers into the silky mesh. God, what was she meant to do next? If Harriet had been there...but Harriet wasn't there. A neighbour had taken her for her physio appointment and she wasn't due back for another hour at least.

An hour could be too long, Lucy thought...

She had punched Santiago's private mobile number into the phone before she had even consciously registered what she was doing.

'I don't know why I'm ringing—you're probably busy and—'

The pleasure Santiago felt at the sound of her husky musical voice—he had never imagined that a woman's voice could give him so much pleasure—was swiftly replaced by anxiety as he registered the uncharacteristic panic in Lucy's tone.

'I am not busy,' he said, closing his laptop as he glanced out at the distant helicopter that was at that moment disgorging suited figures, black blobs in the distance. He had flown them in for the meeting he had already cancelled twice because he was working his schedule around his love...sex life.

The mental correction smoothed the indent between his dark brows. A sex life he could handle; a love life was too high maintenance.

The chemistry between them was so strong that he had been confident that the fire would burn itself out quickly, but if anything it was stronger than it had been. And despite the combustible raw quality of their lust she still managed to make him laugh in bed and, even more amazingly, out of bed, but then Lucy was, as he was discovering, an incredibly smart woman and unlike the other smart women he knew she seemed remarkably undriven.

Lucy swallowed. 'I don't know why I'm ringing you,' she admitted, 'but I didn't know who else and you...' She stopped, thinking, *Whenever I feel bad or am in trouble your voice will make me feel better...* Was that part of being in love?

Her knees sagged and she sat down heavily. Luckily there was a chair there to break her fall. *Oh, God, Lucy, you idiot!*

'I am glad you did. Now take a deep breath and tell me what is wrong.'

Other than the fact I've fallen in love with you? she thought, before taking the suggested deep breath and laying the facts out in a voice that showed a marked tendency to tremble... Her voice never trembled.

How could she be in love with someone she didn't even like a lot of the time, someone she had originally hated? Admittedly she'd never been indifferent to him, for Santiago was not a man who inspired indifference. Respect, yes, and admiration; she had seen this with her own eyes. And she admired him, not because he was rich or powerful, but because he was a man who wanted to be a good father, a man who cared for his younger brother, a man who set himself impossibly high standards and all the time there was that deep sadness she sensed in him... Would he always pine for his lost wife and feel responsible?

The tension that had been holding every muscle in his body rigid loosed its vicious grip as Santiago listened.

'A donkey...this is about a donkey?' A tidal wave of relief washed over him as he banished the images of Lucy in peril that his fertile imagination had conjured.

The suggestion of laughter in his voice brought an angry sparkle to her eyes. 'Are you laughing at me?'

'Not laughing, no…I will be there in less than five minutes.'

Lucy put the dead phone down. As always Santiago was not a man who used two words when one would do, but on this occasion she felt his promise had been optimistic.

She had not allowed for his innovation or his access to expensive toys, she realised as she watched a helicopter put down on a flat area several hundred metres from the *finca*.

Santiago, looking devastatingly handsome, dark and exclusive in a silver-grey suit and dark red silk tie, strode across the meadow to join her.

He did not waste time with small talk.

'Show me the way.'

Inside the stable Santiago took off his jacket, unclipped his watch and rolled up the sleeves of his white shirt to reveal his strong hair-roughened forearms before dropping down in the straw beside the animal.

He ran his hands over the animal, speaking in a soft soothing voice.

'Her name is Bonnie,' Lucy supplied.

'As in Bonnie and Clyde?'

Lucy tipped her head in acknowledgement. 'You look like you know what you're doing,' she said, impressed by the competent way he was gently examining the animal.

He lifted his head and delivered a heart-stopping white grin.

'I'm all you've got so let's hope so, *querida*.' He had seen horses delivered and had helped himself as a boy, but not for years. 'I'm assuming a horse is much like a donkey. Lucy, I need some water and soap.'

She nodded and went away, coming back a few moments later with what he had requested. 'Is there anything I can do?'

'I'll let you know. She's done all the hard work—she just

needs a little help, don't you, girl? I think I should be able to free the legs manually.'

Taking this as a request to keep out of his way, she took a few paces back as he stripped off his shirt and plunged his hands and forearms into the bucket of water.

Lucy lowered her eyes and stared at her hands. She needed a manicure, she thought, extending her fingers, but not as much as she needed a little self-control. Her lustful appreciation of his beautifully muscled back was wildly inappropriate considering the circumstances.

'It's a boy.'

With a gasp Lucy looked up in time to see the new mother nudge her damp baby and begin to clean him as he staggered to his feet.

Tears sprang to her eyes. 'Oh, that's so beautiful.'

'Yes, very beautiful.'

Something in his voice made Lucy turn her head. She discovered that Santiago, who was drying his hands on his very expensive jacket, was looking not at the newborn but at her. She felt the warmth bloom in her cheeks as her tummy went into a deep dive.

She brought her lashes down in a protective sweep to hide the emotions she was struggling to contain. 'You were brilliant. I'm really grateful.'

He tilted his head. 'I do my best.'

Santiago's best was in her experience better than perfect.

'But actually I did little.'

Other than leave a dozen high-powered executives standing watching as he had jumped into the helicopter they had just vacated and ruin a suit in reaction to her plea for help, said the voice in his head.

'It was very chivalrous.'

The women who had shared his bed, the ones he told upfront that the only female he altered his schedule or put himself out for was his daughter, might have called it something else.

Santiago's acknowledgement stopped short of speculating what word his previous lovers might use to describe his actions.

Lucy watched as he pulled on his shirt. On anyone else she might have described the dark ridges along his high cheekbones as a blush but this was Santiago, she reminded herself, dismissing the idea.

'I'm just glad I came back this morning when I did,' she said, her brow puckering as she recalled how close she had come to remaining in bed with Santiago. Where he was concerned her willpower went out of the window.

He stopped fastening his shirt and stared at her. Conscious as he did so of the tight knot of smouldering resentment and dissatisfaction that had lingered in the pit of his belly all morning loosening. 'So you were concerned about the animal—that is why you would not stay.' He had never had a woman refuse an invitation to remain in his bed, but it was not bruised ego or sexual frustration that had made him unable to dismiss the incident—he had virtually begged. Santiago knew his dissatisfaction went deeper.

Accepting now that the root of the problem was he no longer wanted casual, hard for him to think let alone say, the question remained: if a fling with Lucy did not satisfy him, what would?

This was uncharted territory for Santiago and he wanted to sort out his own feelings before he shared his thoughts with Lucy—bring it into the open and there was no going back. Others had paid for the mistakes he had made in the past and he would not allow that to happen again.

It's called scared, mocked the unsympathetic voice in his head.

On the way to his face Lucy's eyes travelled over the

golden expanse of his deeply muscled chest. Things deep in her pelvis quivered as she fought the urge to touch his skin. 'I told you.'

'Did you?' he husked, lifting a strand of silver pale hair from her cheek and watching her bewitching blue eyes darken before he bent his head to touch his lips to the exposed curve of her neck.

Lucy shivered and clung, pressing her face into the angle of his shoulder. 'Yes, I explained.'

'I couldn't have been listening. It is possible, I think,' he slurred against her mouth, 'that I had my mind elsewhere.'

'I wanted to stay,' she admitted as she emerged breathless from a deep, drowning kiss. 'But I...'

He took a deep breath and pulled back from her. 'I know you have made a commitment to your friend and I respect that.' That did not mean it didn't frustrate the hell out of him. 'But the situation will not always be this way. When the plaster is off and you are a free agent...'

Lucy's heart rate escalated. 'Yes...?' she prompted.

'Then we will review the situation.'

The anticlimax was intense... She'd anticipated warm and loving and got a bucket of cold and clinical right in the face, and it was all her own fault for allowing herself to harbour unrealistic expectations because she had fallen for him. That was mad but a fact, and trying to convince herself that he felt the same way would be compounding the insanity.

'Great, I can hardly wait,' she flung carelessly over her shoulder as she picked up the bucket and stalked away, head high, hoping to prove that she could do cold and clinical, too.

Frowning heavily, he caught up with her at the door.

Lucy reluctantly responded to the heavy hand on her shoulder and turned back.

'Have I done something to annoy you?'

Refusing to meet the dark eyes searching her face, Lucy shrugged carelessly, knocking his hand from her shoulder. 'Not a thing.'

Cursing under his breath, Santiago followed her out into the yard. He stopped short, almost colliding with Lucy, who had stopped dead.

'I don't believe this,' he heard her mutter.

'I think in military terms they call this a three-pronged attack.' In personal terms they called it too many people, he thought as he watched his daughter emerge from his estate manager's Land Rover, the vet from his car and Harriet from the neighbour's MPV.

He managed to restrain Gabby until after the vet had examined the new mother and baby and pronounced both to be fit and well. She then dragged Lucy back into the barn. Santiago, who would have liked to drag Lucy back in the barn himself, though not to visit the donkeys, watched as he fielded the seemingly innocent questions being tossed at him by an avidly curious Harriet, questions that made it clear that Lucy had not discussed their relationship with her friend.

Didn't women tell each other everything? He had certainly always operated on this principle, never confiding in bed anything he did not want repeated, but it appeared Lucy was an exception.

He excused himself as quickly as he could politely do so and went back to retrieve his daughter.

Gabby was perched on the rail around the animal stall, watching with starry eyes the newborn foal and mother. Sometimes the overwhelming love he felt for his daughter hit him, rendering him speechless, like a bolt from the blue. This was one of those times—it made all the sleepless nights of worry worth it.

Lucy sensed his presence courtesy of the hairs on the back of her neck before Gabby did. The expression in his beautiful eyes as he watched his daughter brought a lump to Lucy's throat... She felt almost an intruder on a private moment, but before she could look away he turned his head.

Their glances locked.

'That's what I want to be.'

The sound of Gabby's happy voice broke the spell that had held Lucy mesmerised. She realised her hands were shaking and pushed them into her pockets, watching as Santiago ruffled his daughter's hair and teased, 'A donkey?'

Gabby rolled her eyes. 'No, a vet, silly!'

'I'm sure you can be anything you wish, but for now I think we should be getting back and leaving mother and baby in peace.'

'Must we?'

'We must.'

Gabby sighed. 'All right.' She ran to Lucy and hugged her.

Not sure what Santiago's reaction to this spontaneous display of affection might be, she didn't look at him as she hugged Gabby lightly back. Did her undefined role allow for such familiarities?

'And you will come to dinner tonight, won't you?'

This time Lucy did look at Santiago, hoping to convey with her helpless expression that this had not been at her instigation.

'I invited Lucy to dinner,' Gabby announced importantly.

'So I see.'

Lucy could read nothing in his expression. 'I think I'm—'

Santiago's drawl cut across her. 'Good idea.'

'It is?' she said, startled.

Santiago delivered one of his silky smooth smiles. 'I wish it had been mine...' His experience of relationships that involved anything more than sex was rusty, to put it mildly. 'Then shall we say seven for half past?'

Her thoughts spinning in circles of speculation, Lucy nodded. 'Fine.'

'I really like Lucy,' his daughter confided as they walked across the yard.

So do I... His forehead pleated in a frown. 'You do know that Lucy has a life of her own—that she won't be here for ever, Gabby.' A life that did not involve him.

'Why?'

'Well, because...' He stopped. 'She just does.'

Beside him Gabby skipped. 'But not for ages yet.'

'No, not for ages yet.'

When she arrived for dinner at the appointed time it was Josef that showed her into the salon and poured her a glass of wine. She was nursing it when Gabby bounced in.

'I need your help!' she said dramatically.

'So you had an ulterior motive for your invitation.'

'This is serious—I'm talking about my future!'

'Sorry,' Lucy said with suitable gravity.

'I hate my school.'

'You mentioned.'

Gabby frowned at the interruption. 'And I don't want to go back next semester. I've been doing some research and I think this is the solution.' She dropped a glossy brochure in Lucy's lap. 'It's only a half-hour drive, five minutes by helicopter and I could be a weekday border.'

'You seem to have it all sorted.'

'They have an excellent academic record plus a brilliant art department, which is important because that's what I'm going to be, if I'm not a vet...but we won't tell *Papá* that bit yet. Just emphasise the academic stuff and tell him that I miss him like mad, 'cos I do.'

'We...?'

'Well, you really, he won't listen to me but he—'

'Oh, no, Gabby, I'd love to help but I can't. This is between your dad and you. He wouldn't like it if I got involved.'

Gabby's bottom lip began to quiver. 'Please,' she said, channelling beaten puppy.

'I wish I could, Gabby, but you should talk to your dad.'

'What should she talk to her dad about?'

Lucy closed her eyes and swore softly under her breath. This was getting to be a habit—she was going to put a damned bell around his neck!

His daughter snatched the brochure from Lucy's lap and threw it at her father. 'I know you'll say no, but just so as you know my life is *ruined*!' On this quivering note she ran from the room.

'What was that about?' Santiago asked, picking up the brochure. His frown deepened as he read the title page. 'How did she find out about St Mary's?'

'Find out?'

'St Mary's is one of the two schools I've whittled it down to. Well, it was obvious the other place didn't suit Gabby,' he said in response to Lucy's look of surprise, 'so I've been looking at alternatives and this one is close enough for her to be a weekly border.'

'Sounds perfect,' said Lucy, biting her quivering lip. 'How's the art department?'

'Exceptional as it happens. What,' he asked, walking up to take Lucy by the shoulders, 'was all that about?'

'Girls that age have hormones.'

'Dios!' He gulped, looking horrified.

'Nothing a little talk can't smooth over.'

'Later. You are looking very lovely this evening.' His eyes

were slow to rise from her cleavage. 'And I, too, have hormones.' His hormones were telling him to rip off her clothes and throw her down on the rug. His appetite for her remained unquenchable. 'We're not eating for a while...' he murmured.

Lucy was already shaking with desire. 'You have to go and talk to Gabby.'

He sighed and dragged a hand through his hair, casting one last wistful look at her mouth. 'I know...I always seem to say the wrong thing.'

The rueful confidence made her lips twitch. 'You're a great dad, Santiago,' she said, wondering how she could ever have thought otherwise.

'I am?'

She nodded. 'And Gabby is lovely, but she will make mistakes and it won't automatically be your fault.'

Aware that he was watching her with an odd expression, and wondering if he was about to warn her she had stepped over the invisible line she was always conscious of when it came to Gabby, she was amazed when he said, 'One day you'll make a great mother.'

But not for your children! The strength of her sadness was almost incapacitating.

'Wish me luck and remember where we were.'

'Good luck.' She managed to hold back the tears until he had left.

When he returned her smile was in place until he kissed it away.

Lucy emerged from the kiss feeling beautifully ravaged and breathless and, as it turned out, not at all hungry—for dinner at least.

Instead, she took his hand and without a word led him to the secret panel and her own personal stairway to heaven.

CHAPTER TWELVE

'GIANNI and Miranda. It's a family wedding.' Lucy regarded the top of his dark head with frustration. 'Have you been listening to anything I have said?'

Santiago closed the lid of his laptop with slow deliberation and turned his narrow-eyed stare towards the figure by the window. Her attention was directed to the dog who had thrown himself down at her feet.

'That animal should not be indoors. You encourage him.'

Lucy patted the animal and pulled a face. 'Rules are made to be broken.'

'Rules are there to make things function smoothly.' She smiled and for a moment he forgot to breathe. She was backlit by the sun shining in through the window; the light picked out the silver highlights in her glorious ash-blonde hair and he felt his chest tighten... She was the most beautiful and desirable woman he had ever seen.

'So you are leaving this morning?' he said slowly. For the past week he had been convinced that there was something she was hiding from him. Was it this trip, he speculated, and if so why?

His brows twitched into a dark line of disapproval. He was already not in the best of moods as a direct consequence of Lucy spending the previous night, not in his bed, but at the *finca*. This surprise she had dropped on him did not improve it, though it did reveal why she had refused to stay the night. Presumably she had been packing for her trip, a trip she had not even mentioned until it was imminent. His frown deepened in direct proportion to his suspicions.

'I'll be back on Friday before the big day.'

'Big day?'

'Harriet has the plaster off next Monday and we planned to celebrate.' The bottle of champagne was on ice and after that there would be no reason for her to stay.

It was something that on a day-to-day basis she tried very hard not to think about. After all, why ruin the pretty near-perfect present? Since that day weeks ago now there had been no mention of the 'review'. Lucy knew from something Ramon had let slip before he left that Santiago ended all his relationships with a gift… Was his review shorthand for some shiny piece of bling? If so she would, she decided, throw it back at him.

'So soon?'

She couldn't leave.

Half of him resented the pressure to face up to his feelings, yet half of him welcomed the push. He had spent the past weeks enjoying the present and dodging the issue of the future. A future he had never imagined sharing with a woman and now, forced by her shock announcement to do so, he was horrified to realise that he could not imagine a future that did not have Lucy in it.

Losing Lucy would be like losing a limb, losing a vital part of him…the better part!

'So soon' had been pretty much Lucy's own reaction when she had seen the day circled on the calendar.

'Not soon—it's almost two months.'

Two months of going to sleep with her in his arms, hearing her voice every day and night. The thought of not…

Santiago took a deep breath, every fibre of his being reject-
ing the idea utterly.

A silence followed her words.

What did you expect, Lucy? she mocked herself. *That he'd
suddenly discover that he couldn't live without you...? That
he'd beg you to stay with him?*

She knew that for Santiago this had only ever been about
sex. It had started out that way for her, too, but she could
have sworn that over the past weeks it had changed, yet he
never acknowledged the fact while she had foolishly allowed
herself to dream and hope.

'I think Harriet will be relieved. She's resorted to throwing things on the floor to make it seem homely. She calls me
a neat freak.' Her laugh sounded almost realistic.

'You are getting better,' he murmured. 'You no longer
leap out of bed after we have made love to neatly fold your
clothes.'

Do not read anything into it, cautioned the voice in her
head, *but he said made love, not had sex.*

'At what?' she challenged.

He arched a brow and she blushed, drawing a husky laugh
from him. 'I sometimes forget that you were...still deep
down I think you remain the blushing virgin.'

Her eyes fell from his as she tried to hide her disappoint-
ment. 'I really should get going.'

'You are back Friday?' he repeated, thinking, *That gives
you two days to get your act together, Santiago. Two days
of hell without Lucy.*

She nodded.

'Two days—it hardly seems worth it.'

Lucy stared—unbelievable!

This from the man who had flown to Australia the previous week, spent two hours at a meeting and had flown

all the way back, according to him because he had a heavy schedule that week.

His heavy schedule had not stopped him spending all but one of those nights with her and he had not seemed tired. She pressed a hand to her stomach, feeling the deep muscles clench and quiver. The earthy memory of the afternoon he had returned still had the power to make her skin prickle with heat.

She had been standing in the stables at the *finca*, leaning on her broom, feeling a glow of satisfaction as she surveyed the results of her labours, when she heard the creak of the large double doors banging closed. Her first thought was, *They need oiling.* The next was less practical.

As she turned and saw the tall figure whose massive breadth of shoulder seemed to fill the doorway her broom fell with a clatter to the floor. Her hand extended in a fluttery gesture to the silent silhouette.

'Santiago?'

'You were expecting someone else?'

In a state of shock, she was incapable of hiding her delight in seeing him. With a cry she ran towards him. Santiago strode to meet her halfway, swinging her off her feet. As their bodies collided his ravening mouth crashed down to claim her lips.

'Now that is what I call a satisfactory hello,' he growled when they came up for air.

She searched his face. 'You look tired.' Tired but utterly perfect, she thought as her sweeping scan took in the lines of strain bracketing his mouth and radiating from the corners of his incredible eyes.

He lifted a hand to his jaw and grinned. 'Now you know why I never let you see me without my make-up on.'

'Funny...' Lucy's shriek was in the nature of a token protest as he carried her over to the bales of sweet-smelling hay stacked in an empty stall. Her heart was thudding with anticipation as he laid her down and knelt beside her.

'This really isn't appropriate, Santiago...'

'The mouth...incidentally a delicious mouth,' he husked, nipping the full pouting curve of her lower lip. 'The delicious mouth is saying one thing, yet the eyes are saying another... Admit it—you want me here and now.'

If he ever knew how much she was in serious trouble. 'I'm working—'

The rest of her protest was muffled by his mouth as it moved with sensuous silken pressure over her parted lips.

'I thought you liked me being inappropriate...?'

The hand that lay on the juncture of her thighs rubbing her through the denim of her jeans was extremely inappropriate; it was also marvellous. 'I do...' she admitted with a throaty sigh. 'I do, but someone might come in and...'

He had shrugged off the suggestion, looking amused. 'What if they do?' There was no amusement in his dark eyes as he held her eyes, just predatory intent that sent her pulse rate through the ceiling. Without a word he yanked her up into a sitting position, then, taking the hem of her light cotton sweater in one hand, peeled it over her head in one smooth motion. Slinging it over his shoulder, he continued to stare at her with that same soul-stripping, hot intensity as he unfastened the clip that held her hair at her nape and sank his long fingers into the shiny filaments, spreading the soft silky mesh around her face.

Lucy shivered, not because the air was cold on her skin, but because his eyes were hot.

'Nice,' he approved, transferring his scrutiny to the pink lace bra she wore. 'But this is so much nicer,' he added, clicking the front fastening and taking a sharp audible intake of breath as her full, firm breasts sprang free from their confinement.

He bent his head and with a groan took one tight pink nipple into his mouth, causing pleasure that bordered pain to rip through her body.

She sank her fingers into his hair and kept his head there against her breasts until they fell back together on the hay.

It had been barely thirty-six hours since they had had sex, yet as they tore at each other's clothes, their mutual hunger amounted to ravening starvation. He took her as if she were the last drop of water in a desert and he were a man consumed by thirst, driven by it.

And Lucy wanted to be devoured. She wanted to give him what he wanted...to surrender to him and the need thundering through her veins.

Nobody had intruded during the frantic coupling and when later that night she had pointed out his apparent immunity to jet lag he had slid her beneath him in the bed and growled thickly, 'You are my cure for jet lag.'

'Is this something you really need to attend?'

The sound of his cranky voice dragged Lucy back to the present. 'I want to attend. Family is important to me.'

His jaw tightened. *And I am not?*

Shock rippled across Santiago's lean face, drawing the skin tight across his perfect bones. He was jealous that she preferred to spend time with her family than him.

She watched, puzzled, as he began to slide the items he had just removed from his briefcase back into it, his expression abstracted. 'I hope you enjoy yourself,' he said, sounding strange to Lucy.

She nodded, struggling to sense his mood. 'I hoped that you would sort out some help for—'

He cut her off with a wave of his hand. 'Obviously.' She had not even come to say goodbye; she had come to arrange Harriet's care.

'So you are close to this...Gianni?'

She smiled, her face softening. 'Yes.'

'Relative—so what is this Gianni? First cousin?' Santiago had tuned into the affection in her voice and taken an instant dislike to this unknown man.

She was puzzled by the glint in his eyes when he said Gianni's name. 'No, actually he's my nephew, though he's older than me. His dad is my eldest brother. He's marrying the girl who is house-sitting for me.'

When Gianni had spoken of Miranda, the stunning petite redhead she had left in charge of her menagerie, Lucy had heard the pride and love in his voice. Her good wishes had been genuine but tinged, if she was honest, with envy.

'It turns out I'm a matchmaker.' It was only her own love life she had problems with.

'So this is something of a whirlwind romance, then?'

Previously Lucy might have agreed with him, but now she knew that when a person fell in love it was not about timing or intention or even desire for it to happen—it just happened. 'That kind of depends on your definition of whirlwind.' She picked up her bag, began to move towards the door and stopped, turning back. 'Actually I was wondering…there are some seats on the flight and my invite is for "and friend"…?'

He arched a brow and looked at her, saying nothing, and Lucy thought, *Help me out here, will you?* 'Would you like to come?'

There, she'd said it, after spending the last week wondering if she should, and now she had and why not? It was no big thing if he said no.

Who was she kidding? It was a massive thing if he said no! If he accepted, this would be the first time they had been seen in public together as a couple… Were they even a couple? Actually she didn't know, that was the problem and, worse still, she had let the kernel of hope creep in. She had allowed herself to think of a future where they were together.

And you based that on what, Lucy? Sure, she stayed the night here sometimes, she even had a toothbrush in his bathroom and a drawer for her clothes, but it was all casual.

The intimacy, the luxury of not thinking before she acted or spoke, did not extend beyond the bedroom or wherever else they made love. Obviously the sex was incredible, sublime, and under his skilled tutelage she had discovered a passionate part of herself she had never dreamt existed, revelling in the world of sensory pleasures that had opened up to her.

But she was only different up to a point. She had never been able to separate the physical from the emotional and that hadn't changed. For a short time she had, out of a sense of self-preservation, refused to recognise the obvious. She was only able to give herself without boundary or reservation because while she had fallen in lust with him that lust had fast turned to love.

Santiago was the love of her life and the knowledge made her feel more vulnerable than she ever had before. Even at the height of the scandal she had been able to retain an objectivity and respond with a cool restraint to the insults that came her way. With Santiago that was impossible; she felt as though she were stuck in the middle of an emotional quicksand with no way out.

'You are inviting me to this wedding—today.' Santiago's veiled eyes fell from hers.

Well, you wanted to know, Lucy.

Only she hadn't known it would feel this bad!

A look was worth a thousand words—was that a saying or had she just made it up? Well, if someone hadn't said it they should have, she decided as she forced a smile.

It had been a calculated risk but she had always known

that this might be his response. She had taken the risk and now she had to live with it.

'Fine, no problem, don't worry about it. It's short notice, I know, and you're busy.' There, she had not made a scene, she had given him a get out. *Which,* Lucy thought, *is very grown-up and civilised of me.*

She didn't feel grown-up.

'I did not say no.'

She smiled and thought, *But you're going to.*

Santiago flicked his cuff and glanced at the silver-banded watch that circled his hair-roughened wrist. 'Give me fifteen minutes.'

Without waiting for her reply, he walked through the open door of his study and closed it behind him.

He had recovered quickly but she had seen the shock on his face. The humiliating memory of it was going to be difficult to erase. Presumably he needed fifteen minutes to polish the details of an excuse... She saw no reason to hang around to hear it and give marks out of ten.

CHAPTER THIRTEEN

LUCY spotted a space on her third circuit of the overflowing airport car park. With a sigh of relief she drove forward, intending to back into the space when the guy in the car behind her zipped neatly into it.

Lucy, her temper fizzing, jumped out of the car just as the other driver got out. She opened her mouth, but her protest died as the man gave a shameless 'all's fair in love and parking spaces' shrug.

'Oh, what's the point?' she asked herself.

About to get back into the car, she registered that the line of vehicles that had followed her were now honking their horns. She thought, *What the hell?* And, grabbing the bag containing her wedding outfit off the front passenger seat, began to walk away from the car as fast as her legs would take her—Lucy had very long legs.

She had gone a few yards when she was hailed by a uniformed figure who came running up behind her, warning breathlessly that her vehicle would be towed if she left it illegally parked.

She paused, then turned and, with an expressive shrug of her own, tossed the car keys to the official.

His jaw dropped as he caught them.

Lucy waved cheerfully and shouted, 'Feel free.' Before,

shoulders straight, her head held high, she walked confidently down past the rows of legally parked vehicles.

What was the worst they could do—arrest her? Actually
they probably could, but only if they could catch her, Lucy
thought, breaking into a jog as she reacted to the reckless
buzz of angry defiance in her head.

She would get to this wedding if it killed her—or got her
a criminal record. Despite her unease nobody stopped her
and she reached the terminal with time to spare—not much,
admittedly, but she had made it.

Now the pressure was off and she had reached her goal
the adrenaline buzz and anger that had got her this far re-
ceded. The anticlimax left her feeling horribly flat, which
was probably the reason that when she was one off the head
of the line and the departure board showed the one thing that
could stop her now she burst into loud sobs.

'Sorry…sorry,' she said to everyone who stared at her as
she struggled to subdue the mortifying sobs. 'It can't be delayed,' she said when she reached the head of the line.

The woman, unmoved by Lucy's tear-stained face and
wobbly voice, shook her head and, professional smile in
place, recited, 'I'm afraid that—'

'No, you don't understand,' Lucy cut back, struggling
to contain her frustration. 'It can't be delayed. I have to
be there for this wedding…' She stopped. The woman was
not listening, she was already looking beyond her, but other
people were still casting curious glances her way wondering, presumably, who that madwoman was, or maybe they
recognised her?

Lucy blew out a breath, hitched her bag higher on her
shoulder and shoved her hands deep into the pockets of her
designer jeans. She struggled to control the paranoia… *Just
because you're paranoid doesn't mean someone isn't follow-*

ing you, mocked the voice in her head, and the same premise was true of staring and judging.

Let them, she thought, lifting her chin. If she had learnt one thing over the last few weeks it was that she had spent the last four years hiding away under the pretence of embracing a simple life. Well, no more—Santiago might be ashamed to be seen in public with her, but she was not going to hide any more… No more skulking in corners—after all nobody could hurt her more than he had. The fact that she had laid herself open to such hurt did not make it any less painful.

Reacting with a brilliant smile and the approved level of meek obedience a person was expected to display in an airport, Lucy straightened her shoulders and, head high, moved away, mentally doing the arithmetic… How delayed could the flight be before she missed the wedding? The answer was not good news. Her window of opportunity was pretty narrow…an hour and a half, two at the most.

Lucy knew she should ring home and warn them she might be late, but that would be admitting defeat and she wasn't ready to yet. What she needed was some coffee. A caffeine hit would make the world look a less unfriendly place.

She had almost reached the coffee outlet when she caught sight of her reflection in a full-length plate-glass window and stopped, a choking sigh of horror escaping her lips. If people were staring it had little to do with her notoriety and everything to do with the fact the mascara that hadn't formed the comical panda circles around her eyes was smeared in streaks down her cheeks.

She pulled a tissue out of her pocket and began scrubbing at her face, tilting her head to see the results in the glass—not great. Coffee, she decided, scanning the area for the nearest ladies' room, would have to wait until she had managed some urgent running repairs on her make-up.

She had just located the sign she was looking for when

she saw them. They were a prosperous-looking couple, the woman in pearls and Chanel-style suit, presenting a picture of understated elegance but very much the supporting act next to the thick-set silver-haired man looking distinguished in a double-breasted suit and dapper waistcoat.

Shock detonated inside Lucy's head like a bomb, wiping out everything except panic. Her feet nailed to the spot, she stood there shaking as she fought off a wave of faintness, while a disembodied voice in her head screamed—*Run!*

She wanted to respond to the voice but she physically couldn't. She just stood and waited, the awful sense of inevitability lying like a heavy cold stone in the pit of her stomach.

The woman saw her first...Barbara. Lucy had always wondered about her. Did she know the true nature of the man she lived with and simply chose to ignore it? Or was she genuinely ignorant? You read of cases where women lived with men who made a mere serial adulterer look pleasant and claimed they had had no clue, that the man they knew was kind and loving.

There was no question that the woman had recognised her. She coloured visibly through the smooth matt make-up and tugged at her husband's sleeve. Speaking in a loud voice, he ignored her interruption at first, then when he did give her his attention there was impatience in his handsome face.

The woman spoke, stabbing a finger towards Lucy. Too far away to hear what she was saying or even see her face, Lucy could sense her agitation from where she stood. After a few seconds the man's head lifted, his gaze following the direction of his wife's pointing finger.

Then they were walking towards her, the wife trailing a little behind her husband, perhaps less eager for the confrontation.

The scene could have been lifted from one of Lucy's recurrent nightmares except instead of wearing pyjamas and fluffy slippers she had mascara streaked all over her face like warpaint. To Lucy's overheated imagination the crowds seemed to part for the swaggering, self-important figure.

Then as suddenly as a switch clicking Lucy was no longer nervous or ashamed. A weird sense of calm settled over her. She was still shaking but now it was with anger. She had allowed this man to steal part of her life, but no more.

Heart thudding, she took the initiative and strode towards them with purpose. Conscious of her mother's advice of 'it's not what you wear, it's the way you wear it,' she lifted her head, and, hearing a photographer's voice saying, 'Work it, Lucy, give it some attitude, baby,' she put an extra sway into her hips.

Control had been taken away from her once but she was about to take it back. Easier without mascara panda eyes, perhaps, but she was working with what she had, and she had a body. A body that until now she had appreciated on a purely 'it works' level, yet now thanks to Santiago she knew possessed a feminine power.

Panic was not a word or an emotion that he had time for, but when Santiago had come out of his study and found her gone he had experienced something that felt uncomfortably like it. Not that this was surprising...not a word, not a note, nothing. She had vanished.

Fifteen minutes, he had said—was fifteen minutes too much to ask for? His jaw clenched as his initial panic was rapidly replaced by a slow simmering fury. He had spent those requested fifteen minutes rearranging a high-powered meeting that had taken weeks to organise in the first place. Bankers had travelled from several continents to attend and he stood the risk of causing massive offence, not to mention a mountain of ill will, by cancelling.

But he had.

And why? Because he had recognised a turning point in their relationship. Santiago knew about turning points—he normally managed to walk before they occurred. He had seen this one coming but he had made no attempt to avoid it, although he'd assumed he would of course choose the fork marked 'I don't do relationships'.

Then she had asked him, not just for more, but to meet her family. It was almost in his mind a public declaration of intent and, instead of telling him to run away, his instinct had pushed him towards it.

In his experience *things* in life were generally simple, it was *people* who complicated things. However this situation, when you stripped away the detritus, amounted to one simple question, or at least the answer to that question: was he willing to lose her for ever? To push away the woman who had removed the wall of cynicism around his heart brick by brick? She was an infuriating, frustrating mixture of toughness and vulnerability and the idea of living a life she was not part of scared him more than anything in his life had. Just admitting it to himself gave him a sense of purpose, a feeling of liberation.

He had vowed never to put himself in a position where he was responsible for another person's happiness but suddenly that responsibility no longer seemed like a burden, it seemed like a privilege.

No longer afraid to take that step off the cliff in the dark, which essentially was what love was, he had finally faced down his personal demons only to find that the woman who had inspired him to take that leap hadn't bothered to hang around and wait for him.

Had she set out to anger him? What other conclusions was he meant to draw when he discovered that to top it all she had taken a car from the garage?

Her selection of vehicle was not wasted on him. It was

the powerful new addition to his collection, a sports model he had made the mistake of describing as not a woman's car... The comment had elicited an 'anything you can do I can do better' tirade, which he had endured with relative good humour because, as he'd admitted to Lucy, she was probably right.

He did not dispute her ability, but this did not alter the fact that he had no intention of providing the means for her to break her beautiful neck.

As he drove the route to the airport he tensed with each successive hairpin bend he negotiated, half expecting to come across the tangled, twisted remains of the car. He never did, so presumably she had managed to get to the airport in one piece. Once he got hold of her that might change, he thought grimly.

It turned out, when he reached the airport, that his car had also made it unscathed. There didn't seem to be a scratch on it, though the fact it was clamped and sitting behind a tow truck made it hard to be positive about this.

For the first time since he had started this pursuit he smiled, then he laughed, making a passing group of tourists turn and stare curiously.

He pointed at the disappearing tow truck. 'That's mine!'

The explanation caused the group of tourists to quickly move on.

Inside the terminal building Santiago was deciding where to begin his search when he saw the couple, recognising the pair from the articles he had read. A split second later he saw Lucy herself. Her tall, blonde-headed figure was not one that got lost in a crowd. The relief he experienced in that moment was quickly followed by a rush of protective concern as he assessed the situation.

He was moving forward to intervene when he saw Lucy straighten her slender shoulders and advance towards the couple looking like a queen, head held high. Her hair swishing like a silver halo around her beautiful face, she radiated confidence and purpose, a sexy avenging angel. He experienced a wave of pride mingled with lust. Lucy Fitzgerald was many things but a coward was not one of them.

Santiago hesitated, torn between a desire to applaud and an equally strong need to rush in and protect her. He forced himself to stand back.

'Well, well, this is a blast from the past...you're looking good, Lucy.' Feeling the lascivious eyes move over her body like grubby hands made Lucy shudder.

'Denis, don't...come away, she's not worth... I don't know how she has the cheek to be seen in public!'

Denis Mulville cast his wife a look of contempt before turning back to Lucy. 'No hard feelings, Lucy.'

Lucy looked at the hand extended towards her and gave an incredulous laugh. 'Go away, you pathetic little man. There is nothing you can say or do that could harm me.'

Denis looked utterly astonished by her response. His good humour vanished in the blink of an eye, replaced by an air of narrow-eyed menace. As he took a step towards her, pushing his face up close to hers, Lucy grimaced with distaste. The man smelt like a distillery; he had clearly been drinking heavily... It took all her willpower to hold her ground and not retreat from the glittering malice aimed her way.

'My, my, you really have come down in the world,' he slurred. His eyes dropped, his sneer growing more pronounced as he took in her jeans, casual open-necked shirt and flat shoes. 'Not so special now, are we, Miss I'm-better-than-everyone-else? Bitch...I showed you.'

'Denis, please...'

The agonised plea from his wife fell on deaf ears, or at least very drunk ears.

He looked around the crowded terminal and raised his voice. 'Stuck-up little bitch thinks she's a cut above—'

'That is because she is.'

The cool voice cut across the toxic bluster and caused Denis to stagger back drunkenly. He blinked, then seemed to Lucy to shrink as he took in the size and quality of the man who had come to stand beside her.

Lucy gave a sigh of relief and relaxed into the strong arms that came up behind her back.

'And who might you be, friend?'

'I am not your friend and I am the man you should be thanking. If one is going to be knocked out cold in a public place I think it is always far less humiliating if the person striking the blow is a man, not a woman...' His austere expression melded into a tender smile that took Lucy's breath away as it was directed at her.

'Yes, I know, *querida*, that you can handle it, but I think possibly he does not. And a man likes to feel needed.' He felt her tremble and pulled her in closer to his side, fitting her curves into his angles. His voice dropped to a low threatening rumble as he pitched the addition for the other man's ears only. 'If you do not close your filthy mouth I will close it for you.'

'You can't talk to me like that,' he blustered.

Pale except for the twin spots of colour on his fleshy cheeks, Denis's face glistened unhealthily with a layer of sweat.

Santiago arched a sardonic brow. 'But as you see I can. To clarify matters, because I have no wish to continue this conversation any longer than necessary, that is not a threat or even a promise, but simply a fact.'

He turned from the older man, who was opening and closing his mouth like a fish coming up for air, and turned to Lucy, his manner altering again dramatically.

'The private jet is on standby. We have, I think, a wedding to go to…' He nodded towards the unhappy-looking woman and said curtly, 'Madam, you have my sympathy.' Before, a hand in the small of her back, he guided Lucy away.

'Good girl,' he said without looking at her, adding as she began to turn her head, 'Don't look back.' For the first time in a long time Santiago wasn't. His eyes were fixed firmly on the future. 'Just smile.'

'I wasn't going to look back and I don't feel like smiling.' She felt like throwing up.

'Well, you should feel like smiling. You just faced your private demon and spat in his face. You came out on top, Lucy.'

Her eyes widened. 'I did, didn't I? Where are we going?'

'Pay attention, Lucy…private jet?'

'But you weren't serious?' It had been a nice touch and she was grateful that he had played along. 'What I don't understand is how you got to be here just when you did.'

'I'd like to claim psychic powers but actually it was luck and of course a few speeding fines.'

He stopped, turning her around to face him. 'Why do you think I'm here, Lucy?' he asked quietly.

Her heart skipped several beats as the rest of the room, the noise, the crowds, all vanished. There was just Santiago and his warm wonderful smile, his expressive eyes saying things that she could not allow herself to believe.

'Don't look at me like that.'

Santiago rolled his eyes. 'Are they handing out double firsts to idiots at Cambridge these days? For an intelligent woman, Lucy Fitzgerald, you can be monumentally stupid at times.' His hands tightened around her forearms and the mockery faded from his eyes. 'You're shaking like a leaf.' He swore through clenched teeth and gritted savagely, 'I knew I should have throttled the little bastard.'

She flickered a look up through her lashes at his clenched profile. 'It's not him, it's you.'

Santiago swung back to her, a look of shock stamped on his dark features. Frowning, he hooked a finger under her chin, drawing her face up to him.

She was too shell-shocked to think of a lie. 'You make me shake when you touch me.' She winced, half expecting to see his eyes light up with sardonic mockery. They did light up—they blazed, but with a male predatory satisfaction that sent her sensitive stomach into a dive. 'I can't help... Ouch!' she yelped as a passer-by slammed a heavy case into the backs of her knees.

'Sorry!'

Santiago snarled something rude under his breath and sent a murderous glare towards the retreating figure.

'Calm down, it was an accident and no harm done. I'm fine.'

Santiago's dark expression softened into a rueful smile as his glance settled on her upturned face. 'I am not,' he admitted. 'This place, it is impossible...' He stopped, shook his head and, taking her hand in his, said firmly, 'We will continue this conversation when we are in the air.'

'There is really a plane on standby?'

'Yes.'

'Does that mean you are coming to the wedding with me?'

'Am I still invited?'

She struggled against a smile as she imagined the reactions of her family, who had been trying to hook her up with a man for years. They might just break out into spontaneous applause. 'Oh, yes, you are still invited.'

'Then what are you waiting for? It is considered bad manners to arrive late and upstage the bride.'

'Oh, I wouldn't do that. Miranda is beautiful,' Lucy delivered, breathless as she trotted to keep up with Santiago's long-legged stride.

The comment drew a laugh from Santiago. 'And you of course are speaking as someone who is a little homely and plain.' At his most dry, he shook his head. 'Taking humility a little too far. Lucy, you are the most beautiful woman in any room at any time.'

The tribute made Lucy stumble and cast an uncertain look at Santiago's lean, autocratic profile. 'I doubt if Gianni would think so.'

'*I* think so,' he ground out forcefully.

Opening the door to the VIP area, he stood to one side and captured her wide sapphire gaze as she walked past him like a sleepwalker. Helpless to fight the knife thrust of sexual hunger, Santiago shot out an arm just as she had entered the room, then, pulling her back towards him and standing in the doorway, planted a the kiss on her parted lips so hard it bent her body in a graceful back arch.

Then as if nothing had happened he pulled her upright. Her world was spinning, people were staring, and who could blame them? Santiago was straightening his tie as though he had not just ravished her in public... Shaking off the daze, she touched her lips, feeling well and truly ravished but also indignant that he had made such a public spectacle of her.

'Please do not distract me, Lucy, we are on the clock here.'

Lucy's jaw hit her chest. '*Me* distract *you*—' she began, but he was dragging her in his wake and she had a struggle catching her breath, let alone talking.

As soon as the jet lifted off Santiago unclipped his seat belt and stretched his long legs in front of him.

'Now, that conversation we put on hold.'

Lucy regarded him, her sapphire stare steady but wary. She tugged at the open neck of her shirt... Santiago anywhere made her feel breathless. In the confined space of the admittedly luxurious aircraft cabin his brooding presence was pretty much overwhelming.

'Why did you not wait for me? I asked for fifteen minutes.'

'I assumed…'

He arched a sardonic brow. 'You assumed?'

'I assumed there was no point. I didn't think you meant it…I thought…' She threw up her hands in frustration and ran her tongue across the outline of her dry lips. 'There didn't seem much point waiting when you were obviously going to say no.'

'Obviously.'

The sarcastic drawl brought a flush to her cheeks. 'Well, how was I to know?'

'Possibly by doing me the courtesy of waiting.'

'All right, I'm sorry I didn't wait but I didn't think you'd say yes.'

'Then why did you ask me?'

Her eyes fell from his. 'Family weddings when you're an almost-thirty-year-old woman who doesn't have a partner can be pretty dire, people looking sympathetic or worse, trying to get you off with their nephew or brother or recently divorced best friend.' The lie came easier because it was essentially true even though it had nothing whatever to do with her reason for asking him.

'So you invited me to stop you looking like a sad loser? You really know how to make a man feel special, Lucy,' he drawled.

She lowered her gaze and sucked in a deep breath, looking at her fingers clenching and unclenching in her lap. 'All right, I invited you because it's what you do if you have a boyfriend…' Even saying it made her feel ridiculous. She left a space for his laugh and when it didn't come she added, 'I know you're not my boyfriend but we do have…' *Sex, all we have is sex. You're making a fool of yourself, Lucy.* But he was here—that had to mean something…didn't it? 'I suppose I wanted more.'

'So do I.'

Her eyes flew to his handsome face. 'You want more?' she repeated, feeling her way cautiously. 'More sex or…?'

'I have no problem with more sex,' he conceded with a flash of his hard wolfish grin that sent a corresponding stab of lust humming through her body. 'However that is not what I meant.' He looked serious now. His muscular shoulders lifted in a shrug but his grave eyes remained fixed on her face. 'This surprises you?'

'Yes, I thought… It always seemed that you avoided being seen in public with me. I mean, I know my reputation is pretty toxic and—' Her voice broke and she bit her lip. 'So it is pretty understandable.'

Santiago had sat there, his body tense, his face set in a mask as he listened, fighting the urge to interrupt, but the little crack in her voice snapped his restraint.

'Por Dios!' He surged to his feet, looking even taller and more commanding than normal in the limited confines of the luxurious cabin. 'Yes, I did avoid taking you out.' The admission made her wince. 'But it was not shame that made me avoid public places…' He shook his head, his expression reflecting his disbelief that she could think such a thing as he dropped into the seat beside her. 'Not shame, just selfishness. The time we had together was so limited. You spent more time with the damned donkeys than me. When we were together I did not want to share you with other people.'

Shaken as much by the raw intensity spilling from him as what he had said, Lucy, who had been bright red as he spoke, was deathly pale as she stared at him, her wide blue eyes glimmering with unshed tears.

Unable to fight the need to touch her any longer, he turned

in his seat, drawing her hands into his lap. Turning them over, he rubbed his thumb across the small calluses on her palms. The light contact sent the muscles low in her pelvis into quivering spasms.

'You walk into a room and you light it up.' The husky throb of his voice made her tremble. 'People are drawn to you—your warmth, your beauty, your genuine interest in them. *Por Dios*, ashamed?' He gave a raw laugh, the pretence of control gone as he stared into her face. 'I know that when you are beside me I am the envy of all men.'

Tears trickled out of the corners of her eyes and she sniffed, dragging her hand from his to dab them, pushing the tendrils of hair back from her face and tucking them behind her ears with trembling fingers.

'I am not an easy man to live with…'

He was asking her to live with him!

'But you are a strong woman.'

'Is that a polite way of saying stubborn and hard-headed?'

'It is a way of saying not like Magdalena.'

Lucy swallowed at the blunt pronouncement, her eyes filling. She felt the raw pain reflected in his tortured expression in the depths of her soul.

'And you won't let me get away with bullying you.'

Unable to bear the self-loathing in his voice, Lucy laid a finger on his lips. 'Please don't say such things,' she begged. 'I hate it and it's not true. Magdalena had problems that were not of your making and her death was an accident,' she told him fiercely. 'A cruel random act of fate.'

She could see in his eyes that he didn't believe her. He would always, she realised, carry the guilt, though with time and maybe with help from someone… The well of love inside her rose up so intense that she could hardly breathe— she wanted to be that someone there for him.

Santiago's chest swelled as he looked into the fierce blue

eyes raised to his. They swam with tears she struggled to hold back as he framed her beautiful face with his big hands.

'Did you really think I would ever let you leave me?'

The emotion in his voice made the fist of longing lodged in her chest grow heavier. She had never known that love could feel like a physical thing…that it was even possible to love someone so much it hurt.

'I would be a madman and, besides, Gabby would never forgive me. She is already imagining the impression you will make on the other girls when you arrive on parents' night.'

'Oh, God, I'm sorry!' Being in a relationship that extended outside the bedroom was one thing, but she could only imagine how the commitment-phobic Santiago would have reacted to his daughter marrying him off.

His brow furrowed. The way Lucy's mind worked remained a mystery he doubted he would ever solve. 'Sorry?'

'I'll have a word with her if it helps. Young girls often fantasise.' Older girls, too.

'You think it fantastical that my daughter thinks of you as a mother?' he asked, sounding strange.

Lucy struggled to read his expression. 'I think it's lovely of her,' she admitted huskily. 'And I'd like to be a friend to her but—look, I know this is none of my business, but maybe—'

'None of your business? Of course it is your business!' He slapped his hand down hard on his chest and gritted, '*I* am your business. And Gabby, she has friends, she has a father—she needs a mother. I was hoping to be able to tell her that she will have one…?'

It took a few seconds for her to register what he had said. Lucy went ice cold. 'Is that a proposal?'

Outrage made her voice quiver and shake. Not the response he had anticipated or hoped for.

'Is that a no?'

'You're asking me to marry you to give your daughter a mother! Too right it's a no!' she yelled back, furious, because with the cold-blooded proposal he had trampled all over her precious dreams. 'When I marry I want a man who—' She bit her trembling lip and scrunched her eyes closed, forcing tears from the corners. 'I want a marriage that gives me more than a ring. I'd prefer a fling than a cosmetic, convenient arrangement.'

'Fling! What are you talking about? I'm not asking you to marry me because of Gabby. I'm asking you to marry me because I love you!' he bellowed.

Her eyes flew open. Paper pale, she dabbed the stray tears from her cheeks. 'You love me?' she whispered, thinking if volume was any indicator he did. She was amazed no one had come running to see what was happening but she assumed they had been instructed to leave them alone. She didn't imagine many people who worked for Santiago ignored his instructions.

'Why else do you think I asked you? Cancel that question. Next time you'll probably get it into your head that I'm asking because you match my hair and tie?' It seemed safer to leave no room for error, Santiago decided as he took her in his arms, drawing her warm soft body into his and feeling the anger drain from his body.

His smile made her heart turn over.

'You love me…?'

'With all my heart, *mi esposa*…with all my heart.'

She shook her head. 'This doesn't seem real.'

He bent his head and fitted his mouth to hers. Lucy gave a sigh as she pulled back whispering, 'I love you, Santiago.'

When they came up for air she was sitting on his lap and had no idea how she'd got there—being there was enough. Being with Santiago was enough, it was everything.

When Lucy tore herself away from him to change she

found her dress hanging freshly pressed, waiting for her. Slipping it on, she smiled at her reflection. The shift with the ruffles around the neck was a shade paler blue than her eyes. It clung, emphasising the curves of her hourglass figure.

When she returned to the cabin Santiago was in a dark lounge suit, the jacket unbuttoned to reveal a grey tie dark against his immaculate white shirt. He looked sleek and sophisticated and utterly gorgeous.

His face lit up when he saw her. 'Nobody will be looking at the bride. You look absolutely incredible.'

Tears of emotion flooded her eyes. In her opinion all eyes would be on her handsome fiancée. 'God, please don't make me cry.'

'You wish me to be nasty to you?'

Lucy gave a watery laugh. 'About us—do you mind if we don't tell my family today?'

He stiffened, the look of wary hurt in his face bringing her rushing to his side. 'It's not that I don't want to tell them—I do want to,' she declared enthusiastically. 'To yell it off high buildings! It's just today is Gianni and Miranda's day. I wouldn't want to steal their thunder.'

His face cleared and he drew her to him. 'Of course you don't, because you are a kind, thoughtful person with the tendency to put other people's feelings above her own, combined with a desire to steal my prize possessions.'

Her eyes went round as she stepped back and gave a guilt-stricken gasp. 'Your car! I forgot. I'm not sure where it is actually. I sort of…double-parked. There might be a fine…?'

'I will bill you,' he promised.

Hand in hand they left the plane, then Santiago handed her into the waiting limo.

Arriving with Santiago at her side was the proudest moment of her life. He went out of his way to be charming and members of her family who commented on him all said the same thing: *a keeper, Lucy, don't let him go.*

Lucy, who had never cried at a wedding in her life, had tears rolling down her cheeks during the simple ceremony in the flower-decked village church. When the couple exchanged their vows Santiago, who held her hand tight all through the ceremony, looked suspiciously misty-eyed himself.

Like many of the other guests they drifted outside where a band played music and people danced under the fairy lights strung through trees.

The band began to play a slow number and Santiago pulled her into his arms.

'You can dance,' she discovered.

He smiled. 'This was a beautiful wedding.'

'It is, and everyone loves you.'

He stopped circling and tipped her face up to him. 'There is only one person whose love I need.'

'You have it, oh, you have it,' she promised in a voice that throbbed with emotion.

Without warning he let out a war cry and picked her up, twirling her around until she begged to be put down.

Back on terra firma she turned her loving eyes on the man beside her. Lucy's heart swelled with love as she looked at him. 'I don't think any day could be more perfect than this,' she said huskily.

'Our wedding day will be.'

'Don't put your hat away, Maeve—it looks like another Fitzgerald wedding to me.'

Lucy turned with a smile to the aunts walking past and shook her head. 'No, not a Fitzgerald wedding, Auntie Maggie, a Silva wedding, but don't advertise it until this one is over.'

'Why, darling,' her aunt retorted, 'you two have been ad-

vertising it since you walked in holding hands and why not?
Ain't love grand!'

'Extremely grand,' Santiago agreed, his eyes on his bride-
to-be.

* * * * *

Mills & Boon® Hardback

September 2012

ROMANCE

Unlocking her Innocence	Lynne Graham
Santiago's Command	Kim Lawrence
His Reputation Precedes Him	Carole Mortimer
The Price of Retribution	Sara Craven
Just One Last Night	Helen Brooks
The Greek's Acquisition	Chantelle Shaw
The Husband She Never Knew	Kate Hewitt
When Only Diamonds Will Do	Lindsay Armstrong
The Couple Behind the Headlines	Lucy King
The Best Mistake of Her Life	Aimee Carson
The Valtieri Baby	Caroline Anderson
Slow Dance with the Sheriff	Nikki Logan
Bella's Impossible Boss	Michelle Douglas
The Tycoon's Secret Daughter	Susan Meier
She's So Over Him	Joss Wood
Return of the Last McKenna	Shirley Jump
Once a Playboy…	Kate Hardy
Challenging the Nurse's Rules	Janice Lynn

MEDICAL

Her Motherhood Wish	Anne Fraser
A Bond Between Strangers	Scarlet Wilson
The Sheikh and the Surrogate Mum	Meredith Webber
Tamed by her Brooding Boss	Joanna Neil

0812 GEN STD HB

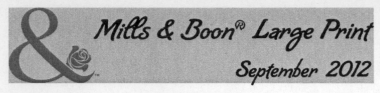

Mills & Boon® Large Print

September 2012

ROMANCE

A Vow of Obligation	Lynne Graham
Defying Drakon	Carole Mortimer
Playing the Greek's Game	Sharon Kendrick
One Night in Paradise	Maisey Yates
Valtieri's Bride	Caroline Anderson
The Nanny Who Kissed Her Boss	Barbara McMahon
Falling for Mr Mysterious	Barbara Hannay
The Last Woman He'd Ever Date	Liz Fielding
His Majesty's Mistake	Jane Porter
Duty and the Beast	Trish Morey
The Darkest of Secrets	Kate Hewitt

HISTORICAL

Lady Priscilla's Shameful Secret	Christine Merrill
Rake with a Frozen Heart	Marguerite Kaye
Miss Cameron's Fall from Grace	Helen Dickson
Society's Most Scandalous Rake	Isabelle Goddard
The Taming of the Rogue	Amanda McCabe

MEDICAL

Falling for the Sheikh She Shouldn't	Fiona McArthur
Dr Cinderella's Midnight Fling	Kate Hardy
Brought Together by Baby	Margaret McDonagh
One Month to Become a Mum	Louisa George
Sydney Harbour Hospital: Luca's Bad Girl	Amy Andrews
The Firebrand Who Unlocked His Heart	Anne Fraser

0812 GEN STD LP

Mills & Boon® Hardback

October 2012

ROMANCE

Banished to the Harem	Carol Marinelli
Not Just the Greek's Wife	Lucy Monroe
A Delicious Deception	Elizabeth Power
Painted the Other Woman	Julia James
A Game of Vows	Maisey Yates
A Devil in Disguise	Caitlin Crews
Revelations of the Night Before	Lynn Raye Harris
Defying her Desert Duty	Annie West
The Wedding Must Go On	Robyn Grady
The Devil and the Deep	Amy Andrews
Taming the Brooding Cattleman	Marion Lennox
The Rancher's Unexpected Family	Myrna Mackenzie
Single Dad's Holiday Wedding	Patricia Thayer
Nanny for the Millionaire's Twins	Susan Meier
Truth-Or-Date.com	Nina Harrington
Wedding Date with Mr Wrong	Nicola Marsh
The Family Who Made Him Whole	Jennifer Taylor
The Doctor Meets Her Match	Annie Claydon

MEDICAL

A Socialite's Christmas Wish	Lucy Clark
Redeeming Dr Riccardi	Leah Martyn
The Doctor's Lost-and-Found Heart	Dianne Drake
The Man Who Wouldn't Marry	Tina Beckett

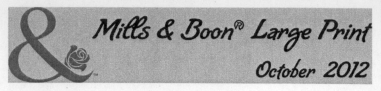

ROMANCE

A Secret Disgrace	Penny Jordan
The Dark Side of Desire	Julia James
The Forbidden Ferrara	Sarah Morgan
The Truth Behind his Touch	Cathy Williams
Plain Jane in the Spotlight	Lucy Gordon
Battle for the Soldier's Heart	Cara Colter
The Navy SEAL's Bride	Soraya Lane
My Greek Island Fling	Nina Harrington
Enemies at the Altar	Melanie Milburne
In the Italian's Sights	Helen Brooks
In Defiance of Duty	Caitlin Crews

HISTORICAL

The Duchess Hunt	Elizabeth Beacon
Marriage of Mercy	Carla Kelly
Unbuttoning Miss Hardwick	Deb Marlowe
Chained to the Barbarian	Carol Townend
My Fair Concubine	Jeannie Lin

MEDICAL

Georgie's Big Greek Wedding?	Emily Forbes
The Nurse's Not-So-Secret Scandal	Wendy S. Marcus
Dr Right All Along	Joanna Neil
Summer With A French Surgeon	Margaret Barker
Sydney Harbour Hospital: Tom's Redemption	Fiona Lowe
Doctor on Her Doorstep	Annie Claydon